FROM: virgilFIB@go2outer.net
SUBJECT: Welcome to the fight!

A message to all our Friends:

FIB reports indicate that The Server has left Earth!
   Now more than ever, we need all Friends to rally around and distract The Tyrant. You will soon receive a message explaining how you can help.
Prepare for the task ahead by:

1. Reading this book. When you find out the color of the Arachnians' venom (in Chapter Two) you will have your first password.
2. Log on to the Outernet by typing www.go2outer. net into your Internet browser, then enter this password to begin your adventure.

   When you have done this, enter your agent ID if you are already a Friend, or register as a new Friend with the FIB. Then check your o-mails — you will receive a message from The Weaver telling you where to find your next password. But remember to open all your other o-mails, and explore your FIB Files and Links before moving on!

   These are critical days. The Outernet needs all the Friends it can get! Stay alert. And remember — be careful out there.

Commander Virgil
Sector Commander, Trojan Sector
FIB (Friends Intelligence Bureau)

**Introducing something truly
out of this world . . .**

WWW.GO2OUTER.NET

odyssey

Steve Barlow and Steve Skidmore

AN
APPLE
PAPERBACK

SCHOLASTIC INC.
New York Toronto London Auckland Sydney
Mexico City New Delhi Hong Kong Buenos Aires

ISBN 0-439-34353-4

12 11 10 9 8 7 6 5 4 3 2 1   2 3 4 5 6 7/0

Printed in the U.S.A.   40
First Scholastic printing, October 2002

FIB ORIENTATION FILE:
FRIENDS INTELLIGENCE BUREAU

THIS IS A TOP SECURITY PROTECTED FILE FOR FRIENDS EYES ONLY. THIS INFORMATION MUST NOT BE COPIED, DUPLICATED, OR REVEALED TO ANY BEING NOT AUTHENTICATED AS A FRIEND OF THE OUTERNET.

)(**Info Byte 1** — The Outernet: The pan-galactic web of information. Created by The Weaver for the free exchange of information between all advanced beings in the Galaxy.

)(**Info Byte 2** — The Server: Alien communication device and teleportation portal. The last such device is in the hands of the Friends of the Outernet.

)(**Info Byte 3** — Friends: Forces who are loyal to The Weaver in the struggle to free the Outernet from the clutches of The Tyrant.

)(**Info Byte 4** — FOEs: The Forces of Evil, creatures loyal to The Tyrant, who seek to use the Outernet to control and oppress the people of the Galaxy.

✴ **Info Byte 5** — Bitz and Googie: Shape-shifting aliens disguised as a dog and a cat, respectively. Bitz is a Friends agent (code-named Sirius) and ally of Janus. Googie (code-named Vega) was formerly a FOEs agent but claims to have defected to the Friends.

✴ **Info Byte 6** — Janus: A Friends agent who, while trying to keep The Server from the FOEs, disappeared into N-space.

✴ **Info Byte 7** — Jack Armstrong: A four-teen-year-old human from England who became responsible for the fate of The Server when it was given to him as a birthday present. Merle Stone and Lothar (Loaf) Gelt: Jack's American friends from the nearby U.S. Air Force base who have been helping him keep The Server safe from the FOEs.

PROLOGUE

The Temple of the Five Winds,
Planet Helios, Trojan Sector
Present day

High on a mountaintop, outlined against the three morning suns of Helios, stands the Temple of the Five Winds: the North wind, the South wind, the East wind, the West wind . . . and the Hoo Past wind. (The mystical wind that blows from the farthest reaches of the Galaxy; the wind that is invisible and proceeds by stealth. On myriad worlds, a faint noise is heard, there is a disturbance in the air, and the ritual cry goes up, "Hoo Past wind?" followed by the solemn, traditional response: "It wasn't me.")

The Temple of the Five Winds looks a lot like the Doric Temples of ancient Greece, such as the Parthenon in Athens. But this temple is a humble affair, consisting of a simple stone rectangle, surrounded by ten tall marble columns. These soar proudly upward, reaching out toward other such pillars that exist on thousands of planets throughout the Galaxy.

The Temple of the Five Winds is the spiritual home to a reclusive group who claim to shun the material world, preferring to travel the planet of Helios on foot with their small earthenware bowls. These devotees beg for alms and commit their lives to learning the mysterious *Way of Kerching* (thought to be named after the sound of a coin hitting a collecting bowl). They are called the Collectors.

From the Temple can be heard the sounds of meditative chanting.

"Sum, sum, sum."

Those who have attained wisdom know that this is one of the Begging Chants of the Apprentice Collectors. There are many others, such as the Chant that is intoned when asking for food ("Yum, yum, yum.") or the Chant of the Hesitant Beggar ("Erm, ahm, um.").

In the middle of the temple sits a shaved-headed, black-robed figure. He is a Master Collector. Squatting around him is a small class of apprentices. Their simple pink robes clash violently with their turquoise-colored skin.

"Sum," chants the Master.

"Sum," repeat his pupils (even the Master's eyes are meditating).

"Sum," chant the apprentices.

Eventually, the Master pauses. He breathes deeply, then nods. The Begging Chant of the Apprentice Collectors is over. It is time for the morning's learning to begin. The apprentices gaze expectantly, ready to hang on to the Master's every word.

As they regard their mentor, a small green butterfly flaps down from its resting place on one of the columns and alights on the Master's shoulder.

Apprentice Dolla sees this and is moved to ask a question that has been bothering him. "Master, is it true what Confusion says, that the flapping of a butterfly's wings can cause ripples in the fabric of the Galaxy, bringing chaos to a planet millions of light-years away?"

The Master is angry. "Silence! Do not speak of that renegade. Confusion is an enemy of the Collectors. He has turned his back on the *Way of Kerching*." The Master violently strikes his shoulder with the flat of his hand.

Splat!

"Chaos brought about by something as small as a butterfly? What a ridiculous idea!"

The Master has no doubts. He knows that the only butterfly in the Galaxy that can give rise to storms powerful enough to flatten forests and cause structural damage to buildings is the Goliath butterfly of Googol, whose wingspan measures more than a mile.

"Confusion was . . ." The Master pauses. A smile passes across his lips. "Confused!"

The apprentices chuckle before the Master silences them with a raised hand and returns to the theme of the day. "And what have my students learned of the mysteries of the Galaxy since our last meeting?" The Master looks around before his magenta eyes fall on one of the pink-robed apprentices. "Speak, Apprentice Dyme."

Apprentice Dyme looks worried. "Ah, Master, we live in interesting times. The Galaxy is in turmoil. The Forces of Evil, also known as the FOEs, led by The Tyrant, are attempting to take over the Galaxy."

"It is even as Apprentice Dyme says, Master," chimed in Apprentice Quarta, who was a bit of a creep. "The FOEs wish to capture a machine called The Server. This will enable them to take control of the Outernet and so achieve their aim. They are in conflict with the Friends, guided by The Weaver, the creator of the Outernet."

"Hold your tongue!" The Master's voice is harsh.

Apprentice Quarta obeys his Master. The apprentice's tongue is a foot in length. He grabs it with both hands.

"Have you learned nothing?" continues the Master. "The *Way of Kerching* teaches us that all conflict is illusion. The Galaxy is illusion! This planet is illusion! Even that thing where a magician places an assistant, dressed in a sparkly costume, into a cabinet and saws the assistant in half is an illusion!" The Master shakes his head. "Apprentice Quarta, you are a young and foolish initiate. To become a true Collector, you must steadfastly follow the Highway of Fuzzy Logic. This will lead to true knowledge."

Apprentice Quarta hangs his head in shame. "I ham thorry, Mathter . . ."

The Master rolls his eyes. "All right, Quarta, you can let go of your tongue now."

The other apprentices snicker.

The morning's lesson continues.

Among the marble columns, the Master recalls stories about Collectors who were once humble apprentices before embarking on the Highway of Fuzzy Logic and becoming greatly revered and much-loved Masters.

He tells the tale of Master Collector Offkeee, who played the accordion and sang songs in an excruciating voice until people paid him to go away.

He tells of the Master Collector Freeloda, who gate-crashed parties and cleaned them out of food and drink before begging for cab fare home.

He tells of Master Collector Frawdster, who collected vast amounts of money for charity, without revealing to the donors that his first name was Charity.

Each of these Masters provides inspiration to the apprentices, who all dream of wearing the black robes of a Master Collector.

As the Master recounts the wisdom of these legendary figures, he is interrupted by the sound of hurrying footsteps. He looks up and sees a pink-robed apprentice scurrying toward him.

"Apologies, Master, but I bring important news."

"Well?"

"It is as Tiresias foresaw, Master." The apprentice cannot hide his excitement. "They are coming."

The Master breaks into a beaming smile. "Excellent! They will bring new knowledge. We must be ready for them. . . ."

CHAPTER ONE

Planet Arachnus III, Fornax Sector

"Spiders," said Loaf. "Uuuugh!"

"They aren't spiders," Merle pointed out. "They just happen to look a little like spiders."

"That's because they have eight legs," said Loaf, gazing at the crowds of aliens moving purposefully through the teleportation station at which he, Jack, Merle, Bitz, and Googie had just arrived. He shuddered.

"Well, yes . . ."

"And they've got those feeler things all around their mouths, and big, staring eyes, and —"

"Why do you have to go by external appearances all the time?" complained Merle. "I bet when you get to know them, they're really sweet guys. You're just prejudiced."

"Against spiders? You bet!"

"They are not spiders!" snapped Merle. "I don't see them weaving webs, their bodies aren't segmented, they must be technically more advanced than we are. The point is . . ."

"The point is," cut in Jack, who had been staring at their surroundings with a growing sense of unease, "where are we?" He looked down at the wirehaired mongrel sitting at his feet.

Bitz gave a doggy shrug. "We're supposed to be on Helios," he said.

Jack nodded, showing no surprise at being spoken to by a dog. He, Merle, and Loaf were used to it by now. Bitz was, in reality, a shape-shifting alien known to the Friends of the Outernet as Agent Sirius. He was also the sworn enemy of Agent Vega, another shape-shifter currently masquerading as Merle's pet cat, Googie.

The cat twitched her whiskers. "I hesitate to question the workings of your razor-sharp *dog* mind, but we read the FIB file about Helios. It said the inhabitants were humanoid. This doesn't look like Helios to me."

Bitz looked worried. "It's not like the Friends Intelligence Bureau to get something like that wrong."

Googie looked unconvinced. "Amateurs," she muttered. Bitz growled.

Merle patted the scuffed plastic case of The Server. "Let's ask Help."

She sat on a seat that had been designed for an alien with eight legs (but hadn't been created for the comfort of any life-form at all) and tapped at the keyboard of what looked like a laptop computer. As Merle and her companions knew, it was nothing of the kind. The device had teleported them to this planet by t-mail. It was an incredibly sophisticated and powerful artificial intelligence that connected them to the Outernet, the pan-galactic web of information.

Jack — along with Loaf, Merle, and two chameleoid companions, Googie and Bitz — was on a mission to return The Server to the creator of the Outernet. Unfortunately, all they knew was this being's name — The Weaver — and that someone on planet Helios could help them in their search.

Merle selected The Server's Help application. A grumpy-looking holographic head appeared above the keyboard and scowled at her.

"Wassamatter now?" it demanded. "You want your noses wiped?" It materialized a holographic handkerchief with red spots. "That was irony," Help explained. "I don't really want you to blow your nose all over me because you'll get mucus in . . ."

"Where are we?" Merle interrupted.

"Arachnus III."

"What are we doing on Arachnus III?" asked Jack.

"Hanging around this dump of a teleportation lounge asking me a load of stupid questions."

"Jeepers creepers!" barked Bitz. "What he means is, why are we on Arachnus III when we should be on Helios?"

"Then why didn't he say so?" Help's expression became preoccupied as it contacted the Arachnian teleportation computer. "That would be," it said at length, "on account of the through-route embargo currently in force galaxy-wide."

Jack gave Help an apprehensive look. "What's a through — whatsit — thingummy?"

"You want a technical explanation?" asked Help. "Or should I just give you the simplified version for cave-dwelling primates?" It gave Jack an insulting leer and began to grunt, "Ugh, ugh . . . egh*ogh,* ugh . . . ugh, ugh, *ogh-ugh,* ugh . . ."

Merle shook The Server viciously. Help gave a startled squeak and rolled its eyes. "Hey, will you watch it? You want to invalidate the warranty?"

"Explain!" snapped Merle.

"Sheesh, what a grouch!" Help's mouth drooped sulkily. "Okay, just don't blame me if you don't get this. The way t-mail works is that your signal is sent via a series of teleportation stations on its way to your destination. Normally, each station just boosts the signal and passes it on to the next in line. That's a through-route. When it's embargoed, it means you can make only one jump at a time. You have to materialize at every t-mail station between your starting point and your destination."

"Just a minute." Merle thought hard. "So it's like going on a train trip — from New York, say, to Chicago — but you can't stay on the train and travel on a direct route. You have to get off at every station on the way — Pittsburgh, Cleveland, wherever — and maybe change trains?"

Help went cross-eyed as it searched its database for information on Earth transportation systems. "Something like that," it admitted grudgingly.

"So who put the embargo on?" asked Jack.

"The FOEs, obviously," drawled Googie. "They're trying to slow us up and get a track on us."

"Then we'd better keep moving," said Jack. "How many stations do we have to go through to get to Helios?"

"Helios is in the Trojan Sector." Help hummed to itself as it calculated. "Maybe three or four, depending on the route and . . ."

"So what are we waiting for?" Loaf was making himself as small as possible to avoid the jostling crowds of Arachnians.

"Do we have to set new coordinates?" asked Merle.

Help shook its head. "No. You'll just move on automatically to the next station."

"Well, there's no point in hanging around." Merle hit the SEND command. . . .

The five travelers arrived on a teleportation pad and gazed at the eight-legged aliens scuttling about their business with brisk efficiency.

"Spiders," said Loaf. "Uuuugh!"

"They aren't spiders." Merle stepped off the pad. She smoothed her jacket and gave Loaf a disapproving look. "They just happen to look a little like spiders."

"That's because they have eight legs." Loaf's scowl and slouching posture were accentuated by his worn baseball cap and grubby New York Giants shirt. In contrast, Merle's fashionable neatness only added to her appearance of being alert and ready for anything.

"Why do you have to go by external appearances all the time?" complained Merle. The dark skin of her forehead furrowed as she gave Loaf an angry look. "You're just prejudiced."

"Against spiders? You bet!"

"Where are we?" cut in Jack. He wasn't feeling too comfortable among these eight-legged aliens, either, though he didn't want to admit it to Merle. She was pretty touchy about any suggestion of prejudice.

Bitz put his head on one side. "This should be Helios," he said uncertainly.

Googie sniffed. "It doesn't look like Helios to me."

"Let's ask Help," said Merle, sitting down and tapping at the keyboard of The Server.

Help appeared. "Now what? I already told you monkeys . . ." It stopped and did a double take on its surroundings. "What are we doing back here?"

"What do you mean, back here?" asked Merle. "We only just got here."

"But you only just left here!" protested Help.

"Hey, Byte-Brain!" said Loaf diplomatically. "How can we be gone from here when we just got here? You can't leave someplace before you arrive."

"I didn't *say* you did." Help was indignant. "You got here, then you left here, then you got here again."

Jack's green eyes were troubled. "Then how come we don't remember being here before?"

"How should I know?" snapped Help.

"Maybe it's because you're a primate with a bad case of arrested evolution and the attention span of a half-witted tadpole!"

"Never mind the insults," said Merle sternly. "Where are we?"

"I just told you that!"

"No, you didn't."

"I did, too!" Help's hologrammatic head did a little dance of frustration. "I told you we were on Arachnus III, and you asked why, and I explained — in my usual helpful way and with incredible patience — that there was an embargo on through-route teleportation, and you said what's that, and I told you it meant you couldn't be through-routed at intermediate stations on the way to Helios. . . ."

"You mean it's like a train trip where you can't travel on a direct route, you have to stop at every station —"

"We went through all that!" Help's eyeballs rotated in opposite directions at high speed. "Enough of this dumb conversation! Will you quit stalling an' t-mail us all outta here?!"

Merle glanced at Jack, who shrugged and then nodded.

She selected the SEND command. . . .

*   *   *

Eight-legged aliens milled around the travelers as they stepped off the teleportation pad.

"Spiders," said Loaf. "Uuuugh!"

"They aren't spiders," Merle told him. "They just happen to look a little like spiders. . . ."

Help groaned. "Oh, shoot — not again!"

The Prison Planet of Kazamblam, Wolf Sector

For a being who was about to deliver some bad news to The Tyrant, Tracer was in a surprisingly calm mood. Not so for his huge companion. The Big Bug, chief of The Tyrant's most notorious band of enforcers, was in a state of terror. Its thick gray hide was pale, and it trembled in every fiber of its muscle-bound body. It knew what happened to beings who failed to carry out The Tyrant's wishes.

Its predecessor, for instance, had been vaporized. It had been one of the lucky ones. The Big Bug's last mission had been to capture the only remaining Server in Friends hands. It had not been achieved.

Tracer was less terrified at reporting this

news to The Tyrant, as he intended to employ the galaxy-wide maxim, "When in trouble, always blame someone else."

The FOEs Chief Surveillance Officer absentmindedly scratched at its elephantlike ears with one of its claws. "The Tyrant is going to be less than delighted with YOUR failure. It was *your* plan. You suggested that we should infiltrate the air force base on Earth and hold the human Merle Stone's father for ransom, forcing her friends to give up The Server."

"But it was *your* plan to use that terrible Arcadian security guard to watch Agent Sirius, and it took its eyes off the ball — all *six* of its eyes!" countered the Big Bug.

Tracer's VR visor sparked violently. "The plan was perfect! It was the implementation that was at fault! Let me remind you that the humans *did* return to Earth from planet Deadrock with The Server. It should have been a simple matter for your agent to overpower them and take control of the device."

Before the Big Bug could reply, there was a series of beeps from the console at which Tracer sat. It was time to report to The Tyrant.

Tracer's six arms became a frenzy of activity as he pushed buttons, plastered down strands of unruly ear hair, and adjusted his visor. The Big Bug gulped and stood stiffly, staring at the large wall screen that began to flicker to life.

A series of static crackles soon transformed into an indistinct dark shadow. The Tyrant, leader of the FOEs and Most Evil Being in the Galaxy, never revealed his identity, even to his senior officers.

"Greetings, O Evil Grimness," cried Tracer, managing with the skill of long practice to grovel in a sitting position.

"Never mind the pleasantries." The Tyrant's voice was as grave as the fate that awaited those who displeased him. "How is the mission proceeding?"

Tracer knew it was futile to lie to his master — he had no doubt that The Tyrant already knew of the humans' escape. You didn't get to be the Galaxy's Most Evil Being by not knowing what was going on. Tracer knew perfectly well that his every move was watched.

"Well, Most Hateful Maliciousness, due to the incompetence of our Bug agents" — the

Bug glared hard at Tracer — "I have autho-rized a change of tactics."

"You?" The Tyrant's voice was a mixture of contempt and threat.

Tracer's calm manner began to crack. "Er, yes, Your Terribleness. This change of tactics will bring more desirable results. . . ."

"How, exactly?"

Tracer's three hearts began to beat wildly. "More desirable results by . . . er . . . not only bringing The Server into our control but also enabling us to capture The Weaver!" These words were greeted with deafening silence. Beads of fluorescent orange sweat broke out on Tracer's brow. He knew he was taking a big risk. As no one knew who or what The Weaver was, his proposal was audacious in the ex-treme. Finally, The Tyrant spoke.

"And how is this feat to be achieved?"

The Big Bug smiled, enjoying the black hole that Tracer had created for himself.

"Well, Your Noble Evilness," stuttered Tracer, "while the humans were on the planet Deadrock, we captured the one named Lothar Gelt. . . ."

"And was this human reformatted to the ways of the FOEs?"

"Not exactly, Your Despotic Disagreeableness. We found it to be unnecessary. The human was already as cunning, cowardly, treacherous, and motivated by self–interest as we could desire. We couldn't improve on the original."

"A creature after my own hearts." The Tyrant's voice was almost wistful.

Tracer continued. "Instead, we implanted a tracking device into the base of what passes for his brain. I am able to trace him wherever he goes in the Galaxy. Should the situation demand it, we can also use this device to exert mental control over him, using the atrocious MindMelt technique that I learned from the unwholesome priests of Uuuur before Your Fiendishness wiped them out. I am sure he will lead us to The Weaver."

The Big Bug gave Tracer a scornful glance. "And just how do you expect to capture The Weaver?"

"*You* will capture him with the help of the information I will pass on to you," snapped

Tracer. "Be ready for action. The plan will work, unless your Bugs fail again."

"If the plan is a sound one, they won't!"

"Enough!" The Tyrant's voice took on an even harsher edge. "Spare me your petty squabbles." There was a silence as the dreaded creature considered. "Your proposal is not unsatisfactory," The Tyrant said at last. "We will try your plan. I look forward to hearing of a successful outcome in the very near future."

Tracer tried to salute with all six arms at once. "Yes, Your Wickedness."

"But remember . . ." — The Tyrant's voice was soft but full of menace — ". . . that into every life, a little rain must fall. If you fail me, prepare yourself for a monsoon."

CHAPTER TWO

Planet Arachnus III, Fornax Sector

"What do you mean, we've been here before?" asked Merle.

"Twice now!" Help had calmed down a bit. It was beginning to suspect that there was more to this situation than the boneheadedness of organic life-forms. "We teleported here, then we teleported out, then we were back here, so we tried to teleport out again, and we still came back here!"

"That's crazy!" sneered Loaf. "I've never been here before. If I had, I would never have come back to a place that's crawling with spiders. . . ."

"I keep telling you," said Merle furiously, "they're *not* spiders. . . ."

"Excuse me."

The companions turned. One of the eight-legged inhabitants of Arachnus III stood directly behind them. It was wearing garments that, judged by their dullness and conservative cut, seemed to be some kind of uniform. It was carrying what looked like an electronic clipboard.

Jack drew back automatically. He was allergic to uniforms, especially as they made his own hand-me-down clothes look even shabbier by comparison. Suppose this alien accused him of making the teleportation station look messy and threw him out? He ran his fingers nervously through his dark hair in a vain attempt to look more like a bona fide galactic traveler. But the Arachnian was apparently unconcerned with Jack's appearance, and it seemed friendly enough.

"I couldn't help noticing," the alien said, its soft voice being automatically translated by The Server, "that you seem to be in need of assistance — may I offer my services? I am a guide with the Tourist Department here on Arachnus III."

Jack willed himself to speak and explained the problem. "So, you see, Help says we've been here twice before, but we can't remember it," he finished.

Having compound eyes with no eyelids, the tourist guide couldn't blink with astonishment, but it managed to convey the impression that it was doing so. "This is most strange and unexpected. Could your application be in error?"

Help bristled. "Listen, eight eyes . . ."

The Arachnian raised four of its "legs" in a deprecating gesture. (Looking closer, Jack saw that its four front limbs ended in manipulative hands. Mainly, it seemed to use the four at the back to move around.)

"Apologies," said the Arachnian. "We will look into this."

Merle, in spite of her convictions, was finding that the spiderlike appearance of the locals also gave her the heebie-jeebies. So her voice was extra friendly as she said, "We're really in kind of a hurry, and it looks like our own t-mail" — she glared at Help, who scowled back ferociously — "is malfunctioning. Could we use your teleportation facilities to get to our next destination?" She made the secret sign of the Friends as she was speaking.

The tourist guide didn't appear to notice the signal. At any rate, it did not return it. "Unhappily," it said, "most of our outgoing teleportation pads are configured solely for the use of my species. We have few visitors here, and the pads we keep for the use of offworlders are currently — ah — off-line. I shall instruct our engineers to undertake immediate repairs. In the meantime, I hope you will accept our hospitality."

"Hospitality?" Loaf's eyes lit up. "You mean, like — food?"

"We have facilities that will replicate items to satisfy all your requirements for food and drink."

"I wouldn't be too sure," said Merle dryly. "You don't know Loaf's requirements!"

In spite of Merle's cynicism, the Arachnian was as good as its word. Two hours later, the humans were so full they thought they might burst. The Arachnian food replicators seemed to have an inexhaustible database of recipes. After sampling their saliva, the machines had produced a continuous stream of delicacies, each more tempting and mouthwatering than the last. Merle and Jack had admitted defeat and lay back in comfortable armchairs, massaging their groaning bellies. Googie (who had complained about her food but nevertheless licked her plate clean) was washing herself, and Bitz was munching happily at a replicated ham bone. Only Loaf, who had already eaten twice as much as Jack and Merle, was still snacking in a sluggish way and channel-surfing through holographic television programs showing a variety of incomprehensible alien dramas and game shows.

Merle, who had been watching Loaf closely, turned to Jack. In a low voice, she asked, "What's your guess? Is he or isn't he?"

Jack was feeling relaxed and sleepy. "Is he what?"

"You know what I mean. Has he been reformatted?"

Jack stretched luxuriously. "I don't know. We'll just have to watch him and hope for the best."

Merle was still looking worried. "What are we supposed to do when we get to Helios?"

"Find 'the sightless one who sees all things,' I guess. That's what Janus said we had to do." Jack's eyelids drooped.

"Hey, Rip van Winkle!" snapped Merle. "Wake up! We've got to figure this out."

Jack sighed, giving up the idea of a nap. "I guess you're right. Okay. Janus told us to find this 'sightless one,' but he didn't say who — or what — it was."

Jack pondered the message they had unexpectedly received from the Friends agent Janus. They had believed Janus to be missing in N-space, a region where matter was thought not to exist. But Janus was clearly still alive in some form and had managed to speak to them through The Server. Unfortunately, the message to go to Helios and find the mysterious 'sightless one' who could lead them to The Weaver had been broken and incomplete.

"There's no point worrying," Jack continued, yawning. "I daresay we'll find out what it's all about when we get to Helios."

"Well, I'm in no hurry." Merle snuggled down farther into the soft cushions of her chair. "We've been zapping around the Galaxy like maniacs for days — we deserve a break.

The guys on this planet may not be Friends, but they seem pretty friendly — and the food here is great! The lamb chops!"

"The ice cream!" agreed Jack.

"The raw liver!" said Bitz dreamily. Merle and Jack gave him disgusted looks. "Hey," the dog protested, "I don't complain about what you eat."

Merle gave a lazy chuckle. "I don't know about you, but I could happily stay here for a few days . . . weeks . . . months, even. . . ."

There was a clatter as Loaf threw the remote control at the viewscreen of the holo-TV. "These shows are the *worst*," he complained. "Isn't there a sports channel or something?"

"Loaf," said Merle wearily, "aren't you ever satisfied?"

Loaf ignored her. "Where's the guy with the extra sleeves in his suit?" he demanded sulkily. "Isn't he supposed to be looking after us? I'm going to find him and get us a little action here. . . ." After three tries, Loaf eased himself out of his chair and waddled across the room to a door set in the opposite wall.

Jack groaned. "I'd better go after him."

"Let him go." Merle wrinkled her nose at

the closing door. "He can be someone else's headache for a few minutes."

Jack hesitated, then let himself fall back into the comfortable embrace of the chair. Merle was right, Loaf could look after himself for a while. "I wouldn't mind the trip to Helios taking a little longer," he said, "if every planet on the way is as welcoming as this one."

"Pssst!" Merle looked around — and groaned at the sight of Help floating above the keyboard of The Server. "I thought I quit you," she complained. "What do you want?"

"Yeah, well, lucky for you, you didn't." Help's voice was uncharacteristically subdued. It scanned the room warily before continuing. "I think we have a problem."

Merle pulled a cushion over her head.

"You mean the teleportation problem?" said Jack casually. "Relax. It's just a slight holdup. I guess there are glitches with t-mail out here the same as there are with e-mail back home."

"Maybe," said Help. "But that wasn't what I had in mind. Did you monkeys read the FIB file on Arachnus III?"

Jack raised his eyebrows. "No. Why?"

Bitz sat up. "I think maybe you should," said Help.

Jack tapped at the keys for a few moments and read the text that appeared on The Server's screen. He gave a low whistle.

"You're right, that doesn't sound too good." He felt annoyed. He'd just gotten comfortable, and now Help was bugging him. "Merle, take a look at this."

With a sigh, Merle sat up and read the screen over Jack's shoulder. Her brow furrowed.

"I don't like the sound of this. Help, can you explain why we kept getting sent back here when we tried to teleport out?"

"No," snapped Help. "I already told you, there's no logical explanation, unless . . . uh-oh."

Bitz pricked up his ears. "Uh-oh, what?" Even Googie stopped washing herself and looked inquiringly at the hologram.

"Weeelll," said Help slowly, "theoretically, it's possible to set up a sort of reverse Chain. . . ."

"Meaning what, exactly?" asked Jack.

"A normal Chain blocks incoming teleports. A reverse Chain would allow incoming traffic, but it could be set up to reflect some outgoing teleports — for instance, any traffic involving non-Arachnians — back to where they started from, creating a t-mail loop. There must be some kind of time loop involved as well, because you didn't remember your earlier visits. . . ."

"But you remembered being here before," Jack pointed out.

"Yeah, okay," snapped Help. "I haven't figured out all the angles yet. Gimme some time, will ya?"

"Are you saying," said Merle slowly, "that we may have fallen into some kind of trap?"

Before Help could reply, a hoarse croak sounded from the doorway.

"Guys."

Jack, Merle, Bitz, and Googie turned to see Loaf standing by the open door, his face pale, his eyes wide and staring with shock. "There's something you ought to see."

Merle frowned. "Not now, Loaf, we're busy."

Loaf didn't move, and he didn't raise his voice. "You really, really ought to see this."

With an impatient gesture, Merle quit the

Help program. She picked up The Server and went to join Loaf, followed by the others. Walking like an automaton, Loaf led them down a series of corridors. "I couldn't find anyone," said Loaf in a hollow voice, "so I started opening doors, and I found this."

They stopped at a door. Loaf pushed it open and signaled the others to go in.

The room was a clinical white and very cold. There were things hanging from the ceiling.

No, not things, Jack corrected himself, staring in shock. *Aliens. People. Many different species of creatures.*

There were hundreds of beings in every shape and form. They were cocooned in strands of white fiber and suspended, frosted and immobile, swaying gently because of the disturbed air caused by the opening door.

Bitz growled deep in his throat. Googie hissed. In a trembling voice, Merle said, "What is this? Some sort of morgue?"

Some instinct had already told Jack what this place was. He fought down the waves of horror that threatened to overwhelm him. "It isn't a morgue," he said, amazed at his own calmness. "It's a cafeteria."

"Oh, no." Merle put a hand to her mouth. "You mean all these poor creatures t-mailed onto this planet . . . ?"

"And got trapped in a teleportation loop, just like we did," said Jack flatly. "And got the welcome wagon, just like we did, and got to eat all their favorite foods, and got fattened up . . ." He looked significantly at Loaf.

"I hardly touched a thing!" wailed Loaf, shaking with fear. "Maybe if I stick my fingers down my throat . . ."

"Shut up," snapped Merle. She looked down at Bitz. "But didn't anybody notice these people were missing?"

"There are billions of t-mail events in the Galaxy every day," whined Bitz. "A few go astray, who's going to notice?"

"Fine. Any suggestions?"

"Er . . ." said Bitz. "Run?"

"Sounds good." Merle flung herself at the door and sprinted down the corridor with the others in pursuit. They skidded around a corner cartoon-style and screeched to a halt.

Facing them were a half-dozen Arachnians.

Their leader, the tourist guide, said, "You should not have left your quarters."

"Yeah, well, we just went for a little walk, you know?" Merle said bravely. "It's all cool, okay? We'll be going back now to eat some more of that great food. . . ."

She got no further. Their benefactors arched their lower bodies forward. White sticky, silken cords shot from spinnerets between their lower legs. With uncanny nightmarish speed, the Arachnians skittered around the helpless travelers, swarming across walls, the floor, and the ceiling as they wove a cocoon around their helpless captives.

As soon as the humans and their chameleoid companions were fully bound, the leading Arachnian reared up to its full height. His eyes bulging with shock and terror, Jack watched as the creature advanced. Poison fangs slid out from beneath its horrible mouthparts and dripped viscous green venom as it stalked toward its defenseless victims.

The Prison Planet of Kazamblam, Wolf Sector

Tracer was worried. The tracking device planted in the human was not working properly. He had tracked Lothar Gelt from Earth to a planetary teleportation station, but there was something wrong. The human seemed to be teleporting *from* the station, but instead of progressing on his journey, he kept going *back* to the station.

This strange glitch was also stopping Tracer from using the MindMelt technique to control the human. It wasn't good. Tracer chewed nervously at one of his claws and began checking the route records again.

Deadrock to Earth . . . Earth to Arachnus III in the Fornax Sector.

A pulse of light flashed across Tracer's visor. Arachnus III? Surely not . . .

The communications chief barked an order to one of the computer terminals. "Files. Information on a planet. Fornax Sector. Arachnus III."

The screen was immediately covered in green pulsing symbols.

As Tracer read the information on Arachnus III, a nasty smile spread across his face. "Oh, dear, those spiders," he murmured. "Up to their t-mail loop tricks again." Tracer shook his head. In the past, The Tyrant had overlooked the Arachnians' "indiscretions," but this was different. This was endangering the success of Tracer's mission.

Tracer clicked on a video intercom.

The Big Bug's features stared out from the screen. "Yes?"

Tracer's reply was measured and firm. "Report here immediately. I have a little job for you. . . ."

Planet Arachnus III, Fornax Sector

The Arachnian stood poised, ready to strike.

A high-pitched chittering resonated down the corridor. It sounded artificial and slightly echoey, as if it were being produced by some sort of loudspeaker system. The Arachnians stopped dead in their tracks.

The humans and their companions watched in amazement as the creatures turned their heads left and right, clicking and gesticulating at one another. Then, as one, they turned tail, completely ignoring their would-be victims. They scuttled down the corridor at high speed, rounded a corner, and disappeared out of sight.

There was a stunned pause. Then Jack, almost gagging with relief, began to tear at the sticky ropelike silk binding them. Bitz gnawed at the material with his teeth, sneezing at the taste. Googie writhed and clawed her way clear. Wriggling and squirming, Loaf and Merle eased their way out of the cocoon.

Jack stared down the deserted corridor. "Where did they go? And why?"

"Who cares?" Loaf, his face set in an expression of disgust and loathing, was trying to pull strands of sticky rope from his clothes and skin. They stuck to his fingers. He gave Merle a furious look. "I think we've all learned something here today," he said savagely. "Eight-legged aliens who look like weird and scary giant spiders aren't always 'really sweet guys when you get to know them.' Sometimes they really are weird and scary giant spiders!"

In the arrivals hall of the teleportation station, the tourist guide and its troops stumbled to a halt, staring in horror at the smoke-filled chaos. Bugs were pouring from the teleportation pads. They were all carrying a variety of lethal weapons and didn't look in the mood to sample the local hospitality.

The leading Bug lumbered to a halt in front of its trembling Arachnian hosts.

"Hello, spiders," it said. "You've been very naughty. I'm afraid you've made The Tyrant extremely angry."

The Bug lifted its weapon. "Prepare to be squished."

Merle dragged clinging strands from the casing of The Server and opened it. "Help!"

"What happened to you?" demanded the moody hologram. "You look like you got in a fight with a cotton-candy machine."

"Shut up." Merle's voice was flat and savage. "We need to get out of here before Incy Wincy and his pals come back. What happens if we teleport to the Helios coordinates?"

"You'd just get caught in the t-mail loop and end up back here again." Help must have decided that Merle was not in a mood to be played with. "You wouldn't even remember all this happened."

"That's what I thought. So what do we do?"

Help considered. "I guess I could finagle

your t-mail signatures to fool the teleportation loop into thinking you're Arachnians. Then you'd get through — but not if you use the Helios address. They'll be watching any traffic to those coordinates very closely."

"Do it," said Merle. "We'll use new coordinates."

"Allow me." Googie, her blue fur streaked with white, leaped onto Merle's lap and patted The Server's keyboard with deft paw movements.

"Hey," protested Jack, too late. "Where are you taking . . ."

His voice was cut off as the t-mail was sent. With a flare of blue-white light that lit the corridor from end to end, Jack and his companions vanished.

CHAPTER THREE

Planet Kippo VI, Epsilon Sector

". . . us?" concluded Jack. Fighting down the nausea that always accompanied travel by t-mail, he blinked and looked around.

They were standing on a low hill, one in a range that stretched to the horizon, just visible in the faint orange light. Jack turned. Behind him, a city lay in a fold of the hills. Twinkling lights shone from windows and illuminated lines of streets.

He looked up. A ringed planet — a gas giant — hung low on the horizon to his left. The rest of the sky was completely dark. There wasn't a star in sight.

"I guess it must be cloudy," said Merle, as though reading his thoughts.

"Cloudy! Ha!" Bitz's furious yap startled

them both. "Cloudy is right. Clouds of interstellar dust. We're in the Coal Sack Nebula."

"How do you know?" asked Merle.

"Because I know exactly where this treacherous, flea-ridden, mange-faced feline brought
us." Bitz was so furious, he could hardly get
the words out. "We're on Kippo VI, which just
happens to be her homeworld!" The fur on
Bitz's neck was raised, and his lips were drawn
back in a ferocious snarl.

Googie skipped lightly out of his way.
"Why act so surprised, dog-breath?" she
taunted. "I've never made any secret of the
fact I wanted to go home. I've not taken you
far out of your way. You can go on to Helios,
and I wish you the best of luck. Have a nice
day!"

Merle stared at her pet in dismay. "You
mean you're staying here?"

"Absolutely I'm staying here. Don't think I
haven't enjoyed being patronized, petted,
given food that would sicken a cockroach, and
dragged around the Galaxy against my will by
a crazy canine and a bunch of know-nothing
humans, because I haven't."

"Oh, yeah?" demanded Bitz. "So you want

us to wave good-bye with a happy smile? And what happens to us when you report to Kippan Security? You think I've forgotten that you people are mercenaries in the pay of the FOEs? I suppose you'll just forget to mention that you came here with the four fugitives right at the top of The Tyrant's most wanted list?"

"What do you think?" sneered Googie. "I haven't been paid for months. You think I'm going to pass up a ticket to the good life? Guess again."

Bitz gave a howl of rage. "I'm gonna tear you to pieces!"

"You'll have to catch me first!" Googie arched her back, stretched . . . and *changed.*

Merle, Jack, and Loaf, who had never seen a shape-shifter transform before, found the process spellbinding (and a little sickening). Googie's muzzle stretched. Her ears grew longer and became pointed. Her neck and body both lengthened, and all four legs became longer and thinner — almost pencil-thin. Her tail shrank to a stump, and her coat shortened and changed color from blue to mottled green with a black stripe down each flank. There was nothing of the cat left in the creature that frisked before them, taunting their powerlessness to interfere.

"Do you think changing to an Altairan bouncing gazelle is going to help you?" Barking furiously, Bitz hurled himself at Googie. Instantly, the dainty creature shot away, bounding high over the uneven ground with huge, improbable leaps, easily outpacing the panting, dog-shaped chameleoid.

"Aw, let the stupid thing go," said Loaf sourly.

Merle turned away from Jack. Her shoulders were shaking. Jack knew that she was grieving for her lost pet. Even though it had been a shock for Merle to learn of Googie's real nature and the chameleoid had made no effort to spare her feelings ever since, Merle had been attached to her "cat." Jack felt helpless. He reached out hesitantly to pat Merle on the arm, but she pulled away and took a few steps down the hill. From the corner of his eye, Jack saw that Loaf was opening his mouth to say something unsympathetic. Jack shot him a look that made Loaf think again.

Bitz returned, his tail between his legs.

"Why'd The Server give me this form?" he whined mournfully. "Why did I have to be a short-legged runt? Couldn't it have made me a greyhound or something?"

Merle gave Bitz an accusing glare. "I thought you said Googie couldn't shape-shift anymore!"

Bitz gave her a hangdog look. "I didn't think she could! She couldn't change form while we were on Earth."

"Well, she's shape-shifting now like anything!"

Jack peered down the hill but could no longer see the fleeing chameleoid. "Can't we catch up with her?"

Bitz shook his head, panting. "Not a chance. The lights down there are Circe City. It's the capital of Kippo VI, her hometown, and just to make things really peachy, that's where the headquarters of the Kippan Secret Service is. There's no chance we can head her off. All we can do now is get out of here before she leads the FOEs straight to us."

Jack sighed. "I guess you're right. Merle?"

Merle turned a tearstained face to Jack and opened her mouth to say something. Then she shut it and nodded.

"Loaf?"

Loaf shrugged. "I never wanted that dumb cat along in the first place."

"Okay." Jack opened The Server. "Help."

Help appeared. "I suppose you want to t-mail out of here?"

"That's right."

"Work, work, work," complained Help. "Figure out new coordinates for Helios, pick up your mail, run antivirus scans, compact files . . ."

"Wait a minute," said Jack. "Did you say something about mail?"

"What? Oh, yeah, you got new mail — didn't I mention that?" The o-mail button on the screen began to flash.

"No," said Jack pointedly, "you didn't."

"So fire me. It's from the FIB. You want to read it or not?"

Seething, Jack selected the o-mail icon. Help vanished into The Server, and a message appeared on the screen. Jack read it. "It's from Commander Rarch. He's chief Friends agent of Epsilon Sector."

"Yeah?" said Loaf in a couldn't-care-less voice. "What's he want?"

"It's a notification to all Friends agents." Jack looked up at Merle. "It's about Googie."

"Googie?"

"Agent Vega, they call her — just a minute, there's an attachment." Jack opened the file. "It looks like a wanted poster of some kind. . . . Oh, no."

Merle gave Jack an apprehensive look. "What is it?"

Jack read from the screen. "It says she's wanted by the FOEs. . . ."

"Let me see that!" Merle snatched The Server away from Jack and scanned the screen. "That's terrible! They've put her on their most wanted list —"

"Yeah?" Loaf brightened up. "Why?"

"Desertion, dereliction of duty, and fraternizing with the enemy — I guess that means us. . . ." Merle turned a frightened face to Jack. "She doesn't know about this! She'll go marching in there, expecting a ticker-tape parade and a congressional medal. . . ."

"And what she'll get," said Loaf brightly, "is jumped by a load of FOEs who'll turn her into fur mittens."

"We've got to do something!" wailed Merle.

"You're right," said Loaf. "We've got to get away from here while they're chasing the cat — or whatever she is right now."

Merle gave him a horrified look. "We can't leave her!"

"She made her wok," said Loaf callously. "She can fry in it."

"Shut up, Loaf." Jack stood gazing down the hill toward the lights of Circe City.

Loaf twitched in his sleep.

Bitz had insisted they wait until dawn before proceeding to Circe City. "You'll be too conspicuous," he'd warned.

Merle had laughed bitterly. "Of course we will — we're human."

"Not because of your shape — you're among shape-shifters, and I've seen weirder forms than human! But Kippans don't move around much before sunup. Get some sleep before we hit the city."

So now Jack, Loaf, Bitz, and Merle were sleeping fitfully on the short, tickly grass of the bare Kippan hills.

As Loaf slept, a voice crept into his mind. *"Lothar! Lothar! Yoo-hoo!"*

Loaf turned over and in his sleeping mind said, *"Just five more minutes, Mom. . . ."*

"Good guess, but wrong." Tracer's voice, from half a galaxy away, echoed through Loaf's dreams. *"Tracer here. I'm contacting you via a MindMelt."*

"MindMelt?" said Loaf. "What's that?"

The answer was a shocking blast of sensation. Loaf felt as though molten lead had been poured into his ears, instantly frying his brain.

"Gnnnnnnnnnnnnnnnnnnnnnn!" he moaned between clenched teeth.

"Shut up, Loaf!" Merle's sleepy voice complained from the darkness. "Go back to sleep."

"That's why it's called a MindMelt," said Tracer in what was left of Loaf's sleeping brain.

"Good name," Loaf's mind answered.

"Just a short, low-level burst to ensure your cooperation." Tracer's thoughts sounded cheerful. *"So there you are on Kippo VI. How unfortunate. The Kippans are an unreliable bunch and very touchy. Once they've captured you, they might just decide to sell you to the highest bidder. And if we intervened to seize*

you, they might change sides and work for the Friends. No, I think on the whole, we'd better move you along. What is your ultimate destination, by the way? Oh, do say, 'I'll never tell you, torture me all you like, you'll never learn the secret from me.' Please do! Then I can have some real fun with the MindMelt."

"Helios," said Loaf hurriedly.

"Spoilsport." Tracer sounded half pleased and half disappointed. *"Oh, well. I suppose I'd better arrange for you to get there."*

"But we can't leave Kippo," Loaf's sleeping mind protested. *"Jack and Merle won't go without Googie."*

"Yes, the timing of that announcement about Agent Vega was unfortunate." Tracer sounded annoyed. *"That's huge, brutal, totalitarian regimes for you. The left claw never seems to know what the right claw is doing. Well, we'll just have to think of a way to help you all escape."* Tracer's tone became flattering. *"I'm afraid I'm going to have to ask you to be both brave and clever."*

Loaf shuddered and made a distressed snuffling noise in his sleep.

"*Yes, I know,*" said Tracer soothingly. "*It goes against the grain. Nevertheless . . .*"

For quite a long time, Loaf continued to twitch and moan unhappily.

"*You have your instructions now,*" Tracer said at length. "*When you awake, you will know what you have to do, but you will remember nothing of this conversation.*" The distant voice began to fade. "*Nighty-night, sleep tight, don't give the Bugs an excuse to bite. . . .*"

The rising Kippan sun woke Jack. He went through all the early morning business of remembering who he was, where he was, and what he was doing there. Then he sat up.

"Come on, Merle," he called. "Morning. Time to go. Come on, Bitz. Come on, Loaf. . . ."

Jack stopped. He stared at the spot where Loaf had gone to sleep, his jaw hanging open. Merle followed his gaze, put her hand over her mouth, and backed away. Bitz barked and hid behind Jack's legs.

After a while, Jack said weakly, "Loaf?"

Loaf blinked at him through bleary eyes.

Jack turned to Bitz. "That is Loaf, isn't it?"

Bitz gave an uncertain growl. "I guess it must be."

"Loaf," said Jack faintly, "you're a pig."

Loaf bristled, shaking his head and squinting his eyes at Jack.

"I don't mean you're acting like a pig," said Jack carefully. "I mean you've turned into a pig. Well, something piglike, anyway."

"A swamp-dwelling stinkhog from the planet Flub, to be precise. If you ask me," said Bitz unkindly, "it's an improvement."

Merle held her nose and made a disgusted noise in her throat. Loaf's new body was making its presence smelt with an odor straight from the inside of a zombie's sneakers. Even by hog standards, the creature Loaf had become was ugly, from the tip of its blubbery purple snout to its ridiculous lime-green tail. Its bright yellow spotted skin bulged with layers of flab, and its three tiny eyes glowed red with malevolence.

Loaf frantically shook his head from side to side, trying to see his own body. Then he hoisted himself up on to his six hooves and raced around in circles, squealing hysterically.

"Loaf!" yelled Jack. "Knock it off!" He attempted to calm Loaf down while the nightmare porker tried to bite him. Bitz raced around, barking wildly and getting under their feet.

When he finally had Loaf under control, Jack panted, "Now what are we going to do?"

"This shouldn't be happening," whined Bitz. "The cat, yes — but you humans aren't shape-shifters!"

"I don't understand it, either," said Jack. "Merle, do you have any idea what's going on?"

There was no reply. Jack stood up and stared around frantically. "Merle?"

"Down heeere."

Jack looked down and gulped.

Bitz said, "Jeee-hoshaphat!"

Something that looked vaguely like a seal with a bird's beak and wings squatted on powerful-looking flippers, looking up at Jack with reproachful eyes. It ruffled its feathers.

"What's that?" Jack whispered to Bitz.

The dog shook its head. "Besides a flying fish's worst nightmare? Nothing I've ever heard of."

Merle screeched. "What's heeeappening to eeeus?"

"That's what I want to know," said Jack. "Help!"

"Yeah? What gives?" Help stared at Loaf and Merle. "What's with the livestock?"

Fighting to keep his voice steady, Jack explained what had happened to Loaf and Merle. "And what we're all wondering," he said, beginning to panic, "is why?"

Help leered at Loaf. "He doesn't look all that different to me." Loaf let loose with outraged squealing. "All right, all right," said Help wearily. "Organic life-forms, go figure, always obsessed with appearances."

"Look," said Jack, "can you just explain what's going on? I mean, I know this is a planet of shape-shifters, but we're just visitors. We shouldn't be able to change shape just because the local life-forms can. . . ."

"That's true," conceded Help, "unless . . ."

"Unless what?"

"Ssssh. Lemme process. I'll see what's in the FIB files. Kippo VI . . ." Files flashed up on the screen as Help mused to itself. "Chameleoid life-forms . . . planetary fauna . . . hmmm . . ."

Jack gave a gasp. He felt as if a surge of electricity had shot through every fiber of his body. For a moment, nothing more happened. Then he felt a terrible pain in his temples, as though his head were splitting in two. It was some moments before he realized that this was, in fact, what was happening. His vision cleared and his hearing sharpened as a new eye and ear grew on each head. One head was set forward on a flexible neck, the other — on a separate neck — was looking backward. Jack realized that the shaggy, bearlike body beneath the heads was his own. He gave a groan and stamped with powerful paws, leaving deep imprints in the springy moss of the hillside.

"Jack!" Bitz gave a frantic bark. "Not you, too!"

"Of two minds about something?" inquired Help in a very *un*helpful way. Jack gave a roar and raised a huge paw threateningly over the hologram.

"Do you want heeeim to tear you chip from chip?" demanded Merle, flapping her wings, "or are you goeeeing to tell us what's heeeappening?"

Help scowled. "I don't take orders from no poultry." Jack roared again, shaking his heads threateningly. Bitz growled. Merle screeched and pecked viciously at the hologram. "Okay," said Help hurriedly, "keep your feathers on. Kippans are pretty secretive about themselves, but according to the FIB files, the latest research suggests that they aren't actually shape-shifters."

"Of cooourse they're shape-shifters," growled Jack's first head.

"Everybody knows that!" grunted Jack's second head.

"Not by themselves. They're actually pretty normal organic life-forms. But on this planet, there's another life-form. The details are unclear, but Friends scientists think the second life-form is a symbiote. It's a kind of virus that lives within the bodies of the Kippans. They give it a form and protect it, and in return, it plays hopscotch with their DNA, allowing them to change into virtually any organic life-form that has the same mass."

"So what yooou're saying," rumbled Jack, scratching his forward-facing head in thought, "is that these sym . . . sym . . ."

"Symbiotes," supplied Help.

". . . have infected uuus, too?" concluded Jack's second head.

"It's a theory that fits the facts," said Help smugly.

"Never mind whether it fits the facts," yapped Bitz, "what do we do about it?"

"Ah," admitted Help sadly, "there, I'm afraid, you have me!"

"You meeean weee could be stuck like this?" asked Merle.

"And if that happens, we can't teleport away from Kippo," rumbled Jack. "We won't be able to get to Helios. We have to find Goooogie and get her to help uuus get back to our own forms — otherwise, we'll be stranded here forever!"

Circe City, Kippo VI, Epsilon Sector

"Ah, Agent Vega," said Googie's supervisor.

On reaching Circe City, Googie had immediately reported by televisor to the Kippan Security Service. She had prudently declined an invitation to the headquarters of the K.S.S. Although she had no idea that she was on The

Tyrant's most wanted list, Googie wasn't nearly as sure of her welcome as she had pretended to Bitz and the others.

After all, she had been sent to Earth at The Tyrant's expense and on his orders and had stopped sending reports back to the K.S.S. when the FOEs stopped paying her for information. Their argument had been that Googie's information wasn't very interesting to The Tyrant as it had consisted mainly of complaints about being cuddled, being made to wear ribbons, being expected to play with a fake-fur mouse, and sleeping in a wicker basket.

Googie's point of view had been that her superiors should try being a cat for a while and see how they liked it. She'd managed to get herself attached to Merle, whose father, Colonel Stone, was in charge of a very important wing of the most powerful military force on Earth, thank you very much, and if she hadn't told the FOEs anything about The Server, that was because there was nothing to tell — so too bad. Thus, by the time The Server had shown up (with the Friends agent Sirius in hot pursuit) and Jack's father had given it to Jack for his birthday, Googie was in

a fine state of the sulks and hadn't even noti-
fied Kippan Security that the device was on
Earth. She guessed that this hadn't enhanced
her popularity or her career prospects with her
superiors.

So she'd agreed to meet her K.S.S. boss in
a public park. The weather was fine, and all
around her, fellow Kippans were enjoying the
warmth of their giant yellow sun by changing
into forms best suited to take advantage of it.
The park lakes were full of Kippans in the
forms of Hydranian basking goldfish, and the
grass was dotted with the shapes of Oolovian
lazybeasts, hedonistic sandlizards, and bone-
lessly relaxed hepcats from the planet Cooool.

Non-chameleoids are often heard to complain about the impossibility of identifying
individual members of a species that can
change its shape faster than a seventeen-
armed Nummonan nannything can change a
diaper. "It's impossible to tell which shape-
shifter is which," they say. "They all look different to me."

But Googie was able to recognize Kippan
Agent 0008 (licensed to be extremely unpleasant) without any trouble at all, even though

her (possibly ex-) boss was currently in the shape of an Armanian gucci monster (a creature not unlike a Gila monster but much more fashionable). For this meeting, Googie herself had assumed the shape of a Marman saber-toothed mongoose, pound for pound the most ferocious fighting beast in the Galaxy. There was no point in taking chances, after all.

"I suppose," Agent 0008 said, flicking its black tongue in and out in an unsettling way, "that you have come to apologize and ask for your old job back."

"Thaf dependf," said Googie. The six-inch fangs of the saber-toothed creature were giving her problems with pronunciation. "Whaf are you offering?"

"Well now, you're lucky," hissed the K.S.S. chief. "On the menu today we have Unspeakable Torments, Lingering Agony, and the special is Terrifying Retribution."

"Whaf are you talking abouf?" demanded Googie angrily. "I know where The Ferver is. I came here to negofiate!"

"Too late for that," said Agent 0008. "We know where The Server is, too. It's here." The Kippan agent instantly transformed into the shape of a taloned, armored Sissilan slash-slayer. At this cue, a dozen agents hidden nearby did the same. "I'm afraid," Googie's now definitely ex-boss continued, "you have outlived your usefulness.

"The Tyrant says, 'Traitor! Prepare to be sliced!'"

CHAPTER FOUR

"Are yooou sure yooou can track Goooo-gie?" rumbled Jack, lumbering along behind Bitz. The dog was loping through the streets of Circe City, nose to the ground, sniffing as he went.

Bitz paused at a televisor kiosk. "She made a call from here. To her bosses in Kippan Security, I'll bet."

Loaf grunted incomprehensibly and sniffed at a lump of food that someone had dropped on the pavement. Jack guessed that it was some kind of Kippan fast-food product. It was clearly a couple of days old and looked like roadkill, but Loaf ate it, anyway.

"There ain't no justice," Bitz complained with uncharacteristic bitterness as he sniffed at the ground around the kiosk to pick up Googie's trail. "I mean, here you are, three life-forms who evolved opposable thumbs and then took *forty million years* to learn how to make a stone axe — you come here, and suddenly you can shape-shift. That good-for-nothing cat comes back here, and *she* can shape-shift. I'm the only life-form around here with the ability to shape-shift all by myself, and I can't change my form to save my life!"

"Shape-shifting," grumbled Jack, nibbling at his shaggy coat with his backward-facing head, "yoooou can keep it! It's a looot mooore trooouble than it's wooorth. First chance we get, we get hooold of Goooogie. Then we find ooout hoooow to get rid of these symbiooootes and t-mail ooout of here!"

Bitz sighed. "Come on, Miss Piggy," he said to Loaf. "Your smell's already sending real estate prices down in this neighborhood." Ignoring Loaf's indignant squeals, the dog picked up Googie's scent and trotted off. Jack (carrying The Server in one huge bear paw) signaled to Merle's seal-bird shape, circling high above, and set off to follow Bitz, with Loaf in bad-tempered pursuit.

*   *   *

In the park, Googie was starting to realize that she'd miscalculated.

"I'm on The Tyrant's moft wanted lift?" she said. "Fince when?"

"Since a couple of days ago. And as our organization depends on His Vileness for most of our funding . . ." Googie's boss gave an apologetic shrug and in the same swift movement drew a concealed weapon. He fired it at Googie who was too stunned to move. She felt a wrenching shock — and, moments later, realized that she had reverted to her cat-shape. The symbiote that had bonded with her on her return to Kippo VI had been neutralized by 0008's weapon.

"Don't look so shocked," the Kippan agent said. "You neglected your symbiote while you were on Earth and lost it, so you were unable to change form. You've been declared *parasitica non grata*. Your body will no longer bond with a symbiote, so you are stuck in your present form. We have no intention of facing a saber-toothed mongoose when we could fight a relatively defenseless whatchamacallit from Earth. . . ."

"The name you are searching for," spat Googie, "is 'cat.'"

"How very — brief. Like your future." The Kippan spymaster signaled, and his fellow agents advanced, their armored bodies glistening, their long, razor-sharp talons slicing the air as they closed in for the kill.

But they had never met an infuriated cat before. Googie's teeth and claws weren't the most deadly weapons the Kippans had ever faced, but her bristling fur and savage snarl made them look as if they might be. The Kippans hesitated — and in that split second, Googie was on them, spitting, hissing, slashing at their eyes. Her adversaries fell back.

In the same moment, Bitz, Jack, Loaf, and Merle entered the park.

Seizing her opportunity, Googie broke through the circle of her assailants and streaked toward her former companions.

"What are you supposed to be?" she hissed, skidding to a halt in front of them. "A circus troupe?"

"It's nice tooo see yooou, toooo," said Jack sarcastically.

"Weee've beeeeen infected with Kippan symbiotes," explained Merle.

"No kidding!" sneered Googie. "And I thought you were just playing dress-up! Trust you to come running to me when things get tough."

"And what did you come running to us for?" demanded Bitz with a ferocious growl. "A letter of recommendation? It looks to me as if your friends aren't too pleased to see you."

Googie looked over her shoulder. The Kippans had regrouped and were advancing purposefully. "All right! Get me out of this, and I'll tell you how to get back to human form!"

"Deal," agreed Jack. Loaf grunted piggy approval.

"Weeee'll fight them off," said Merle.

"Not in that form!" snapped Googie. "You couldn't fight off a Rabbian sleekit cowrin timrous beastie! I'll tell you what forms to take. Let's start with Siianese fighting gerbils."

Jack barely had time to say "fighting gerbils?" before his symbiote responded to Googie's command. His heads grew together and merged into one, which was a very strange and unpleasant sensation. His body became round and squat. He grew two tails, and sharp spines shot out from his back. The most dramatic change was to his rear legs and feet, which elongated into powerful limbs ending in long, slashing claws.

Turning, Jack could see that Merle was similarly transformed. Black eyes stared back at him over a twitching nose. They both turned to Loaf.

Loaf hadn't changed into a fighting gerbil. His body was still more or less pig-shaped, but he had lethal-looking tusks on either side of a mouth filled with teeth that looked like white needles, and a bony forehead with three sharp horns.

Googie hissed at him. "That's a Tinugan triceraboar! Fighting gerbil, I said!"

Jack shook his head. "I don't think Loaf can change into anything except a pig of some sort," he squeaked.

Googie gave a disgusted wail. "That figures. I suppose it'll have to do."

There was no time for any more talk. The Kippan agents were upon them.

Jack and Merle quickly found out how to make the most of their bodies' fighting abilities. Their long legs gave them awesome speed and power. They leaped on their ene- mies with great kangaroo bounds, then sat back, firmly balanced on their twin tails, lash- ing out with ferocious claws. The Kippans were unable to get at them from behind be- cause of the sharp spines on their backs.

The battle was evenly matched. There were more Kippans than "humans," but the humans had more body weight and could deal heavier blows. Jack and Merle could take on three or four slashslayers at a time, with Googie and Bitz harrying the others with sneak attacks. Whenever the Kippans tried to regroup, Loaf's triceraboar would make a fero- cious charge and scatter them like tenpins.

The Kippans soon found themselves at a disadvantage. Their slashslayer armored forms were too heavy to be nimble but too light to do much damage. Soon, several of them were looking pretty out of it. Their leader saw the way the fight was going and called them off. There was a whispered consultation.

Jack, panting, turned to Googie. "Okay," he squeaked, "we've driven them off — for now — but we still have to get away from here. . . ."

There was no time for further discussion. Time-out was over. The Kippans were changing.

Jack and his companions stared as the transformation was completed.

"What on Earth are those?" breathed Merle, gazing with astonishment at the portly shapes that were beating their stubby wings furiously in a lumbering attempt to get airborne.

"They're nothing on Earth," said Googie tersely. "They're plummeting tortoises, from the planet Kwikduk."

"*Plummeting* tortoises?" Jack's gerbil mouth twitched into a grin, but Bitz gave a worried growl.

"They're not funny," snapped the dog. "I've heard about these babies. They don't look like much, but wait until they gain some height."

"Why? What do they do?" But even as Jack spoke, the leading tortoise had reached attack altitude. It furled its wings, drew them — and its wrinkled head and scaly legs — back into its shell, and dropped like a stone, straight at Merle. Her lightning-fast gerbil reflexes came to Merle's rescue. She danced sideways — but even so, she barely avoided the attack. With a noise like a basketball hitting wet concrete, the tortoise slammed into the ground, leaving a large crater. Sticking its head, wings, and legs out of its shell once more, the creature gave the startled companions a chilling reptilian stare, then labored to fly again.

"Those things can dive with pinpoint accuracy and crack a four-inch slab of granite!" yelled Bitz. He gave Googie a frantic glance. "Now what do we do?"

"You can quit whining and let me think!" snapped Googie.

Within seconds it was raining tortoises. Soon, there would be too many to avoid. But Googie's desperately racing mind had come up with an answer. "Indanian rubber plant-forms," she yowled.

Jack's gerbil legs turned green and seemed to flow into the soil. His body stretched like a rubber band and sprouted a hundred pliable, fleshy leaves. His eyesight faded.

As they were now plantlike creatures, Jack and Merle could neither speak nor see — which was a pity because they missed Loaf's contribution to the action. His misfiring symbiote had given him the form of a Norcoochian flying pig from the improbable planet of Butbutbut, and he was harrying the ungainly tortoises as they fought to gain height, sending them fluttering to the ground.

However, there were too many tortoises for Loaf to deal with all of them. The majority were still able to reach attack height. Bitz and Googie scurried into the shelter of their friends' protective leaves. The deadly hail of tortoises was unable to break through: The harder the infuriated reptiles hit, the farther they bounced off the springy leaves. The park rapidly emptied as rebounding tortoises whistled over the heads of the noncombatants like fireworks.

At length, the Kippan spymaster rallied his demoralized forces for a final attempt. This time, the attackers became sleek yellow-and-black insects with whirring wings. On the front of each was a sting like a rapier. They formed a circle around the defenders, buzzing angrily. Then they turned tail and shot away.

Googie gave a low growl. "Human," she said.

The rubber plant-forms transformed back to Jack and Merle, who stood blinking in the sunlight.

"We're back in our own bodies!" cried Merle delightedly. "And the Kippans are retreating! We've won!"

"I'm afraid not." For the first time, Googie sounded frightened. "They've transformed into ballistic hornets from the second moon of Ricochet."

"But they've gone away!"

Bitz hung his head in defeat. "They're just circling around to pick up speed. In attack mode, ballistic hornets fly at twice the speed of sound. They can drill straight through armor. I'm afraid we're goners."

Jack stared at Googie in disbelief. "But there must be something we can turn into!"

Googie shook her head. "I can't think of any life-form with a hide thick enough to repel an attack by a ballistic hornet. I thought you'd probably prefer to be perforated in your own forms."

"But can't we t-mail out of here?" said Jack. "Help!"

Help appeared. "I know, I know," the hologram rasped, annoyed, "you want to get off-world: No can do right now. The Kippans have put a t-mail damper on the whole area. I have to neutralize it before we teleport, and that'll take time. . . ."

"Which we haven't got." Bitz looked over his shoulder. "Here they come! It's been nice knowing you guys. . . ."

Bitz was interrupted by a loud and revolting squelching sound. The companions turned — and their jaws dropped.

"What's happened to Loaf?" Merle screeched.

Before anyone could reply, the dripping, wobbling mound Loaf had transformed into rolled forward with terrifying speed, engulfing its screaming (and howling and yowling) companions alive.

Stuck inside the sticky, translucent body of the creature like pieces of fruit suspended in Jell-O, Jack watched in openmouthed horror as the hornets dived in for the kill . . .

. . . and shuddered to a halt as they bored into the insubstantial, energy-absorbing protoplasm of Loaf's transformed body. There they hung, hopelessly stuck, powerless to reach their targets.

Moments later, Merle, Jack, Googie, and Bitz found themselves lying on the grass, coughing and spitting, covered in translucent goo, shocked but alive.

Bitz was the first to find his voice. "An Algolian blob," he marveled, staring at Loaf. "Yow-sah! Absolutely gosh-darned brilliant!"

"I was just going to suggest that," snarled Googie, trying to wash herself everywhere at once.

The Loaf blob was now expelling the hornets who lay, unable to fly, in attitudes of exhaustion and defeat. As the last hornet flopped onto the grass, Loaf began to change back to human form. Moments later, he stood grinning at Jack and Merle.

"Will you look at my keyboard!" said Help in a disgusted voice. The hologram hadn't been affected by Loaf's goo, but The Server had. "Anyhow, I neutralized the damper field:

T-mail is enabled." Help looked around at the spluttering companions. "Well, don't congratulate me all at once." Help retreated into The Server in a huff.

Merle gave a hacking cough. With a cold shudder, she picked up The Server and gave Googie a look that said very clearly that this was one pussycat that wouldn't be getting any supper if Merle had anything to do with it.

"Before anything else happens," she said in a tight voice, "how do we get rid of our symbiotes?"

Googie sneezed. "Oh, that? Easy. I can set the teleport so it only sends our bodies. The symbiotes just get left behind."

"That's *it*?!" Merle looked like she was about to say something else but thought better of it. "Fine. Do it."

Jack opened his mouth — and shut it again. *Let Merle call the shots*, he thought. *This is not a good time to interfere.*

Merle opened The Server. Googie's paws danced across the keyboard. After a short interval, she said, "Done."

"Good." Merle's finger hovered over the

SEND key. She turned to Loaf, wondering if she would ever be able to erase the memory of being absorbed by "the blob."

"Do me a favor," she said in a toneless voice. "No matter how desperate the situation gets, no matter how hopeless the fight, no matter how dim the prospects or bleak the outlook — don't ever, I mean *ever,* do that again!"

Her finger jabbed down. There was a flare of blue-white light as the t-mail converted their atoms into an energy signal that flashed out into the vastness of the Galaxy, heading for their next destination.

CHAPTER FIVE

Space Trading Post 478, Trojan Sector

"Is this Helios?" asked Merle.

The group had materialized in a large concourse lounge. Metallic walls shimmered in the glow from overhead green lighting strips, and a wall of computer screens flashed information in incomprehensible symbols.

"I don't think so," replied Bitz. "It looks like a space station teleport lounge."

"And we've hit it at rush hour," said Jack.

He was right. Hundreds of aliens were standing, floating, or, in the case of some exotic Jell-O–bodied life-forms, in lines that led to a row of desks where officials were checking the identity of the travelers.

The number of different alien life-forms was mind-numbing. There was a multitude of creatures of varying shapes and sizes with skins, hides, and exoskeletons in every color of the multispectrum rainbow of Chromatoid IV (which has so many different shades that paint company executives, on seeing them, invariably burst into tears). Some aliens were wearing clothes, some weren't, and in other cases it was impossible to tell. Some beings had transparent bodies (which meant that their internal organs could be seen bubbling, pumping, and gurgling away), and some had their internal organs placed externally.

There were aliens with hair, aliens with fur, aliens with hairy fur, aliens with no hair and no fur. There were beings with any number of arms, legs, tentacles, and claws. One had such a variety of manipulative limbs (including one that Jack felt almost sure was a can opener) that it looked like some kind of living multipurpose tool. There were androids, insectoids, humanoids, and others that didn't fit into any "oid" category at all. As Jack looked on, more and more creatures materialized in the lounge and headed toward the security desks that guarded the exit.

Even after the experience on Kippo VI, Jack

was still impressed by this variety of life-forms. "Incredible! Who could have imagined this?"

"So what?" drawled Loaf, unimpressed. "There are more realistic-looking aliens in *Star Wars*."

"But that was just fantasy," Merle pointed out. "These aren't jerky computer-generated characters or guys in latex suits. These are for real."

Loaf chuckled. "Well, compared to these nasty guys, the aliens in those movies are *hot*." He turned to Googie. "You're welcome."

Googie gave him a hard stare. "What?"

"Oh, sorry, I thought you just said, 'Thank you for saving my worthless hide back there, you shouldn't have risked your lives for me, I am not worthy.'"

"Go scratch your armpits, monkey!" snapped the cat. "You want thanks? For butting in on me when I was just about to sweet-talk my boss into taking me back with a raise, a promotion, and a health plan?"

"I think a health plan," said Merle caustically, "is supposed to give you treatment when you need it. It looked to me as if your boss's plan was just to leave you needing treatment."

Googie sniffed. "I had the situation well under control until you primates and that tail-wagging idiot dog showed up, so don't expect any gratitude." She gave her companions a look of disdain. "By the way, has it occurred to any of you to wonder why we're not on Helios? I entered the right coordinates."

"Must be another teleport glitch," ventured Bitz.

"Let's try the hologram," suggested Loaf. "It usually has an answer, even if it's the wrong one."

"Before we do that, we'd better move away from this crowd," said Bitz. "We don't want to draw attention to ourselves." There was general agreement, and the group moved away from the lines at the exit to a far wall where they huddled protectively around The Server.

"Help," whispered Jack.

There was a loud *ching* as Help shot out. "WHADDAYA WANT NOW?!" screeched the hologram.

One or two of the aliens in line glanced toward the small group.

"Shhh." Jack glared at the hologram. "Where are we?"

There was a slight pause as Help checked The Server's memory and location files. "Space Trading Post 478, Trojan Sector."

Bitz gave a puzzled growl. "Why aren't we on Helios?"

The hologram blinked as it discovered unexpected information. "Because there's a protective Chain around Helios. All teleports are forbidden. This is the nearest we can get to Helios by t-mail."

Googie was startled out of her sulk. "That's strange. Why would a small, unimportant planet like Helios be protected by a Chain?"

Help shook its head. "Can't say."

"So how are we going to get to Helios?" asked Jack.

"Get a ride!" Help disappeared back into The Server.

"There's no need to be rude," Merle said.

"He wasn't being rude," explained Bitz. "He's right. The only way to Helios will be to get a ride on a spaceship."

Loaf's eyes glinted. "A ride on a spaceship? Wow! Now that is better than fiction!"

"How do we do that?" asked Jack.

"We have to get to the space dock," answered Bitz. "This is a trading post, so there'll be dozens of flights leaving. Some ship is bound to be heading for Helios."

Loaf gave a big grin. "What are we waiting for? Come on!" He started to head toward an exit line.

"Wait!" Googie's sharp command made Loaf stop dead in his tracks. The chameleoid motioned toward the security desks. "There's a problem — we've got to get through there."

Merle looked toward the lines of aliens passing through. "No one is showing any ID," she said.

"It's not necessary," said Googie. "Everyone is given a tri-D scan."

"That's like a photograph, only it's a holo-image," explained Bitz in answer to Jack's clueless stare. "The image is instantly checked against galaxy-wide data files."

"Will we be in the files?" asked Loaf.

"We've stopped The Tyrant getting his hands on The Server," explained Merle wearily. "We're on his list all right. . . . All of us," she said, glaring at Googie for emphasis.

"And I'm not talking about his Christmas card list."

"The Tyrant doesn't celebrate Christmas, birthdays, or anything that has the words 'merry' or 'happy' in front of it," said Bitz. "The only holidays he celebrates are Bad Friday, Forced Labor Day, and Painsgiving."

Merle shook her head. "Doesn't he ever just, you know, have a good time with his buddies?"

"What buddies?" asked Bitz. "Anyway, we're wandering off the point. As soon as the FOEs get a visual of us they'll know we're here. And they *will* have your pictures. Remember, you were in Kazamblam."

Jack gave a shudder — he preferred not to recall the time he, Loaf, and Googie had spent on The Tyrant's prison planet.

"And Loaf was captured again on Deadrock," Bitz reminded him. Jack looked quickly at Loaf, who failed to meet his eye. Nagging suspicion about Loaf rose again to the forefront of Jack's mind. Had Loaf been reformatted to become an agent of the FOEs? He'd saved them on Kippo VI by turning into the blob thing, a creature the humans had never heard of. How had he done that? Jack sighed. Was Loaf a traitor? There didn't seem to be any way of finding out.

Googie was looking around nervously. The cat no longer seemed as sure of herself now that she was a fugitive, too. "We need a plan," she said, "and quickly. We can't stand here much longer — we'll arouse suspicion."

Jack scrutinized the officials standing at the security desks. They were large, one-eyed beings with no hair and smooth green skin. They were dressed in black uniforms and were, like all immigration officials, unsmiling.

"They look pretty mean," said Jack.

"They're cyclopians from the planet Polyphemus. The best immigration guards in the Galaxy," explained Googie. "They've got big eyes to spot any trouble and big bodies to sort it out."

"We'll never get past them without being recognized," moaned Bitz.

"One-eyed guards. That reminds me of something," murmured Jack. He clicked his fingers. "Odysseus!"

"Gesundheit," said Merle. "Oops — sorry, I thought you sneezed."

Loaf gave Jack a baffled look. "What?"

"All this reminds me of part of the story of Odysseus," said Jack. "We studied it at school. It's by Homer."

Loaf snorted. "Don't be stupid! He's a cartoon character."

Jack looked puzzled.

"Homer. D'oh!" Loaf slapped his forehead.

"Not Homer Simpson!" cried Jack. "Homer was a poet in ancient Greece. He wrote *The Odyssey*. It's a story about a Greek warrior named Odysseus who was trying to get home after a war with the city of Troy. It took him ten years to sail back to Greece because he and his men kept getting lost or diverted. They had lots of strange adventures."

"The history lesson is very uninteresting," said Googie snidely. "In any case, what has it got to do with us?"

"In one of the adventures, Odysseus and his men were captured by a one-eyed giant called a Cyclops. It kept them in a cave and started to eat them. They finally escaped by hiding under a flock of sheep."

"Hey, guess what," sneered Loaf. "We've just run out of sheep here."

Jack gave him a cold stare. "What I meant was that we've got to disguise ourselves to get past the cameras and the officials."

"Wanglefish!"

"You too, cat-face," replied Loaf.

"I was just testing whether you are free of the symbiotes," said Googie. "You haven't turned into a Finanian wanglefish, so your bodies must be clear. That's ironic — the one time we need to shape-shift to disguise ourselves, we can't."

"Well, I'm pleased about that," said Jack. "I don't much feel like growing another head again."

Merle snapped her fingers. "Great idea!" she exclaimed. The others looked at her, puzzled.

"The FOEs are looking for five one-headed creatures. What if we give ourselves extra heads? Bitz and Googie can hide under Loaf's shirt — it's big enough. They can stick their heads out and be a three-headed alien! Jack and I can do the same — stick both our heads through his shirt. Then we'll be an alien with two heads and four legs! There won't be any pictures like that in any FOEs files!"

"In a lifetime of listening to dumb ideas," said Googie, "that's the dumbest I have ever heard. In fact, it's so dumb, nobody would dream that anyone would be dumb enough to try it. It just might work!"

"Let's do it!"

Despite Loaf's protests, Merle and Jack helped Googie and Bitz to climb into his shirt. "Stop scratching," howled Loaf. "Ow! When were your claws trimmed? Eek!"

"I'm worried about fleas," said Googie, pushing her head out of Loaf's shirt collar.

Loaf turned his head and stared, nose-to-nose with the chameleoid. He began to scratch himself. "Do you have fleas?"

"No. I'm worried about catching them from you."

Loaf's reply was cut off by Bitz's head butting his chin. Merle laughed. "Now us." She gave Jack an encouraging grin. Jack felt himself turn an interesting shade of red at the thought of being so close to Merle. After some moments of wriggling, Merle succeeded in pushing her head under Jack's shirt and out through his collar.

The "aliens" settled into separate exit lines

and began to shuffle toward the security desks. (Jack and Merle found this difficult as they kept stepping forward with opposite legs, until they agreed in whispers to start walking right-foot-first every time.)

"Stop licking my ear," Loaf hissed at Bitz. "And you should think about using tooth-paste — talk about dog-breath."

"I *am* a dog," Bitz reminded him. "And stop moaning or I'll really make some smells under here."

Loaf stopped walking. "You wouldn't dare!"

"Try me."

Jack and Merle tried to avoid eye contact with any other beings as the minutes passed and they got nearer and nearer to the security desks. To their right, the Loaf creature reached the front of the line and stood next to the security desk. The unblinking cyclopian official stared hard at the monstrosity before it. A camera above the desk zoomed in on the three heads and clicked. There was a long pause as the image was analyzed. All three heads held their collective breath.

WHAAAAAAA! WHAAAAAA! WHAAAAAAA!

A siren blared. Red lights flashed. The ruse

hadn't worked! Beads of sweat broke out on Loaf's brow. Bitz panted. Googie flattened her ears.

The official facing them roared a command, and a metal door whooshed open to reveal more cyclopians. They were all armed with disturbingly large energy weapons. Jack and Merle watched in horror as the guards clattered toward Loaf and the chameleoids. Loaf shut his eyes and missed seeing the cyclopians run straight past him.

At the same moment, a metallic android dodged out of the line behind Loaf and the chameleoids and began running away from the guards. The cyclopians barked a warning. Everyone farther down the line — except for the android and the chasing guards — hit the floor. The humanoid machine clanked hurriedly toward the teleportation area. There was another shout, followed by a series of explosions as the cyclopians opened fire on the fleeing robot.

Merle gestured toward Bitz. The chameleoid gave Loaf a quick nip on the ear. "Run!" he barked.

"Ow!" Loaf opened his eyes, saw Merle

and Jack hobbling toward the exit, and quickly followed. Nobody took any notice of the two strange-looking "aliens."

"Nothing to declare!" yelled Loaf as he scampered past the unguarded desks.

The two chameleoids dug their claws into Loaf's shirt, desperately hanging on, their heads bouncing up and down. The sounds of battle and alarms grew distant as they fled.

Outside the teleportation facility, the companions found themselves in a huge bubble of plastic and metal that seemed to be the hub of the trading post. Within the massive structure, thousands of life-forms hurried through an abundance of malls and promenades. These were connected by moving walkways and shafts into which aliens casually stepped to be effortlessly wafted up or down between the post's many levels.

"Antigravity lifts," Bitz explained as he wriggled out of Loaf's shirt, followed by Googie, who immediately began washing herself.

Jack whistled. "That's some trick." He helped Merle duck out from under his shirt.

She smoothed out her shirt and ran her fingers through her messed-up hair.

"Actually, the trick is providing normal gravity in the rest of the station. We're in space, remember." Bitz sniffed at a metallic object that looked like a fire hydrant and was saved from an embarrassing indiscretion by Jack's startled protest.

"Sorry," said the dog, shamefacedly lowering his leg. "Species memory. It cuts in when I'm nervous." Googie gave Bitz one of her most superior stares.

Out beyond the bubble's clear walls, there was nothing but blackness and stars. Floodlights lit up the dozens of spaceships and star cruisers that were docked at the port. It reminded Jack of a giant yacht marina. Enclosed tubular walkways led to the moored ships and along these, aliens walked, shuffled, and slithered to board the waiting vessels.

"Now this *is* better than *Star Wars*," said Merle.

Loaf nodded in agreement, speechless at the sight of so much technology and wealth.

"Stay here," ordered Googie. "I'll make my

way to the docking area and see if I can find a ship that's going to Helios."

Bitz growled. "Why you?"

"Because I know how to negotiate with spacers, and I don't smell like a dead rat in a locker room."

"Well, hurry up," snapped Bitz. "We don't want to hang around here for too long."

Googie arched her back before turning tail and bounding across the floor. The others found a bench and settled down. Jack set The Server on his knee and watched the space-ships arriving and departing. He wondered where the ships were going to and coming from, what beings they were carrying into the farthest reaches of the Galaxy. He grasped The Server and a flood of anxiety washed over him. How could they ever hope to find The Weaver in such vastness, among so many billions of life-forms?

Hopefully, the sightless one on Helios would give them the answer, he reminded himself. Then they could get back home. Jack shivered as he thought about his mother and father. He guessed they were worrying about him. Other questions flashed randomly through his mind: Could Loaf be trusted? What happened to Janus, and had he guided them correctly? What would happen on Helios? But the one question that kept coming back was "Why me?"

Jack put his worries aside as Googie returned with a strange-looking figure in tow.

"This is our way off here," the chameleoid announced, by way of introducing her new companion.

The outlandish figure held out a grimy, six-fingered hand. "Zodiac Hobo, space desperado, adventurer, pathfinder, wayfarer, and vacation tour operator. Like, greetings, space dudes."

CHAPTER SIX

Space Trading Post 478, Trojan Sector

Bitz, Merle, and Loaf stared wide-eyed at the humanoid figure smiling before them. He had long red hair, a green beard that looked as if things lived in it, orange skin, a shirt with lace frills, a pair of blue wide-bottomed pants, and sandals.

Zodiac winked. "I see you dig my threads." He made a futile attempt to brush food stains off his pants. "Made of plants grown from the very best sun seed. You gotta love my solar flares."

Bitz gave Googie an appalled look. "You're planning on getting a lift to Helios with this space bum? You gotta be kidding."

"He's from the Jivan system. They're all a little laid-back," said Googie defensively. "But he's got a ship. And he's cheap."

"Bargain-basement, if his fashion sense is anything to go by," muttered Merle. "Anyway, what's he going to charge us? And how do we pay him?"

"Don't worry about that," said Googie. "We made a deal."

"Can you take us to Helios, Mr. Hobo?" asked Jack.

"Hey, no 'misters' here. Call me Zodiac. Helios? Helios, shmelios. Easy cabana. Follow me, interstellar groovers. My space rig awaits."

"Was that a yes?" Jack whispered to Bitz.

"Sounded like it. He said he'd take us to see his ship," Bitz replied.

"Can we trust him?" Jack asked.

"Can we afford not to?" Bitz shrugged. "Come on."

The self-proclaimed space desperado led the group through the throng of traveling aliens, down passageways toward the docking area. "So, where do you hang your space helmets, daddios?" he asked. "And, like, what brings you to this neck of the Galaxy?"

Jack shot Merle a warning glance.

"We're tourists from Earth," explained

Merle cautiously. She wasn't going to give anything away.

"Never heard of it. Crazy name, though. Sounds like a blast."

Merle looked puzzled but continued, "We want to see the Galaxy. Get out of Earth's atmosphere and reach for the stars."

Zodiac scratched at his beard. "No offense, dudette, but what d'you want to do that for? Stars are big balls of fire — they'll burn you to a crisp before you get near one."

Merle rolled her eyes. "I was speaking figuratively."

"Yeah? Cosmic." Zodiac brought the group to a halt. "Okay, hipsters, here we are."

"Wow! Look at that!" Loaf pointed at a sleek-looking vessel with impossibly curved lines and shining metalwork. It was everything a spaceship would look like in the wildest dreams of a director making a multi-million-dollar sci-fi blockbuster movie. "Your ship is the *business.*"

Zodiac gave a laugh. "Whoooooeee! Like I could afford a Sensor Wing MKIII Cruise Liner! Even if I wanted a fat-cat, gas-guzzling square mobile like that, it'd cost several million

Galactibucks I don't have." He shook his head. "That ain't my ship. *That's* my ship." Zodiac pointed to a small rust-colored vessel moored beneath the gleaming giant. Its appearance was closer to a junkyard than a spaceship.

Merle groaned. "How did I know he was going to say that?"

"I've seen better-looking insurance write-offs," said Loaf. *"After* they went through the crusher."

Zodiac looked hurt. "Like that crazy cat Confusion says, 'Don't judge a banoobian by its spiny horns and bad breath.' Okay, it may look a little past its fly-by date, but remember, 'A bwarba in your hand is worth two in your pants.'" He marched down the translucent walkway. The others followed. Zodiac cracked the air lock hatch and stepped inside.

"I know The Server's translating what he says," Merle whispered to Jack. "But do you think Help could give us a translation of the translation? And will you just look at his ship!"

"Don't worry," said Jack, adopting a positive air. "Maybe it's like the *Tardis* in *Doctor Who* — one of those ships that's bigger on the inside than it looks on the outside."

It wasn't. It was one of those ships that was even smaller on the inside than it looked on the outside.

Merle gazed around at the cramped interior in dismay. "There's not enough room to swing a cat," she said. Googie gave her a hard glare. "Oops, sorry. It's just a saying. . . ."

Inside, the ship looked as if it had been undergoing a major DIY renovation that had suddenly stopped due to a lack of funds. There were patched-up walls, ripped-up seats, wires hanging out, and — even more disconcerting — a large toolbox under the seat where Zodiac had plonked himself down.

"It might not look like much . . ." the pilot said deprecatingly.

"You're not wrong," muttered Loaf.

". . . but this baby can go from zero to five hundred big ones in a few seconds. Whoosh factor ten in the blink of a cyclopian's eye."

"Cyclopians don't blink," said Googie.

"I was speaking figuratively." Zodiac gave Merle a wink.

"What's your ship called?" asked Jack.

Zodiac looked puzzled. "Say what, wild child?"

"What's its name?" Jack shrugged. "Where we come from, all spaceships have a name."

Zodiac was nonplussed. "Crazy. That's a new one on me. I just call it *Ship.* What do you call ships where you come from?"

Jack searched his memory. "Er . . . *Eagle. Snoopy. Voyager. Enterprise . . .*"

Zodiac scratched his head. "Sounds pretty weird to me. . . ."

"I should think it would!" cut in a metallic voice that somehow sounded tearful. "Why would you bother giving me a name when you just take me for granted all the time?"

"That's my ship's brain," explained Zodiac, giving his passengers a shamefaced grin. "Say hi, *Ship.*"

"Oh, that's right, bring your friends around anytime," whined the voice. "Don't mind me."

"Hey, don't bug me, *Ship,*" said Zodiac. "Whaddaya say we just throttle up and hit the interstellar gas? Destination Helios, Trojan Sector, whoosh factor five."

There was a silence.

"I said, 'Destination Helios, Trojan Sector, whoosh factor five.'"

Still silence.

"Oh, baby, don't get heavy with me!" pleaded Zodiac. "Like, I don't need these negative vibes. It's bad karma, you know? Let's get going!"

"No!" snapped *Ship.* "I told you yesterday, that's it. I'm leaving you. You can find yourself some other artificial intelligence. I'm going back to my motherboard."

"Oh, shootin' stars!" Zodiac banged the console.

"Don't you raise your fists to me!"

All the lights on the ship went out.

"Sorry about the domestic downer, gang," said Zodiac's voice from the darkness. "Guess this is where you cats earn your passage."

"Googie," said Merle apprehensively, "what's he talking about?"

"That's the deal," explained Googie. "He gives us a lift to Helios, we provide counseling for his ship."

"How can a ship need counseling?" asked Loaf. "Ships aren't people. They're machines. They don't have moods."

"Ha!" exclaimed Merle. "Just think of Help."

Loaf considered. "Point taken."

Ching! The hologram's head pinged out from The Server. "I heard that, primate! I am not moody. I am helpful. I always do everything I'm asked."

"Absolutely," said Googie, keeping a straight face. "So you are going to be the counselor, and get this ship to fly."

Help realized it'd talked itself into a job. "Me and my big voice simulator," he muttered.

"Well?" said Googie. "We're waiting."

"Okay, okay!" Help materialized itself a beard, horn-rimmed eyeglasses, a notebook, and a pencil. "Hello, *Ship*. Come in and lie down on the couch." The lights came on.

"There isn't a couch." *Ship*'s voice sounded confused.

"Well, just relax, okay? Take a load off your processors. I want you to think back to when you were just a little silicon chip. Did you love your systems programmer? Did you have a tough time with auto-dump training? What's the problem?"

"It's my pilot," sobbed *Ship*. "He doesn't

appreciate me. I've given him the best years of my run time, and he treats me like corrupted data. He hasn't even given me a name!"

"Oh, what's the deal with names?" groaned Zodiac. "If you want a name, I'll give you a name."

"How about *Pile of Junk?*" muttered Loaf. Jack elbowed him in the ribs.

"What about *Trigger?*" said Merle innocently.

"*Trigger,*" said *Ship* speculatively. "*Trigger.* I like the sound of that. I would love to be called *Trigger.*"

"*Trigger* it is," sighed Zodiac. "Can we get going now?"

"No."

"Aw, comet gas, now what?"

"Hey!" complained Help. "Will you quit interrupting? My client is in a highly emotional state, do you mind?"

"Thank you," sniffed *Trigger* (formerly known as *Ship*). "He doesn't appreciate me."

Help nodded. "I know, I know. Organic lifeforms, don't get me started. Especially primates." Help glowered at the humans. "They only learned to walk upright because they were always trying to reach for bananas and scratch their butts at the same time."

"He could say thank you every once in a while."

"I know, I know. The guy has the manners of a Snabollian snarf-snaffler." Help's voice took on a cunning tone. "How dare he treat you this way, when you can set coordinates in the pulse of a plasma proton."

Sniff. "You bet I can."

"And fly like no other ship in the Galaxy."

"It's true, it's so true."

"I should say it's true!" Help's eyes narrowed. "You know what? If I were you, I'd show him what you can do. Prove that you're the best! Show this miserable humanoid how much he *needs* you. Make yourself indispensable. Show him who the real boss is!"

"You're right! I am, he does, and I will!"

Trigger's engines roared into life.

"Coordinates set for Helios. Watch this! You ungrateful slob!"

With a lurch, the ship blasted off from the trading post and shot into the void. Zodiac's look of bafflement became a grin of delight. "All riiiight! Go, *Trigger*! Yee-haaa!"

Help gave a wink before disappearing back into The Server. "Works every time. Ships' computers — sweet, but stupid."

Deep Space, En Route to Helios, Trojan Sector

As his ship hurtled through the emptiness of interstellar space, Zodiac recounted tales of his adventures. All of these were as incomprehensible as they were unlikely. None of his passengers listened. Loaf and Bitz slept, Googie washed herself, and Merle and Jack were too busy taking in the thrill of this latest experience.

Jack settled back into his seat and gazed at the unfolding vastness of space. The blackness was lit by dots and swirls of yellows, whites, blues, purples, and reds as the light of thousands of stars and distant galaxies flickered and twinkled.

Merle, too, sat transfixed. "We're looking back in time, you know," she whispered.

Jack turned to her. "What do you mean?"

"The light from some of those stars has taken millions of years to reach us. We're looking at history. Maybe back to the actual beginning of the universe."

Jack stared in awe. "Incredible." He glanced across at Merle, who had drawn her knees up to her chin and was clearly brooding. "Worried about your dad?"

Merle nodded sadly. "I know Googie said the FOEs wouldn't try to get at me through him again, but I'm all he's got since Mom died. I guess he'll be frantic by now, wondering where I've gone."

"Send him an o-mail."

"I don't think that would help. Either he wouldn't believe the sender address, or he'd have a conniption."

Jack shrugged. "I guess you're right. In that case, all we can do is get this mission over with as soon as possible and head back to Earth." Merle gave him a wan smile.

Fortunately for their peace of mind, neither Jack nor Merle was aware that their position was being tracked from the device in Loaf's brain or that The Tyrant's chief communications officer was, at that very moment, in contact with the third human in their party.

Tracer's voice echoed in Loaf's sleeping mind. "*Hello again. Nearly there, now.*"

Loaf groaned and twitched in his sleep. "*Not you again! Leave me alone!*"

"*Now, is that polite? Would you like another demonstration of the MindMelt?*"

Loaf's mind cowered. "*What do you want?*"

"*That's better. I must say, I enjoyed your escape from the cyclopians. Your disguises were almost inventive. Of course, you'd have been spotted, anyway, if I hadn't t-mailed a criminal android from its cell in Kazamblam into the teleportation lounge to create a diversion.*"

"*You did that?*"

"*Certainly. Otherwise I would have had to arrange for you and your friends to pass through the cyclopian checkpoint unhindered, probably arousing their suspicions in the process. As it happens, the cyclopians also saved me the job of disposing of the android. Kapow!*" Tracer chuckled. "*As renegades go, you really are a pretty hopeless bunch.*"

Even Loaf could only swallow so many insults without retaliating. *"Yeah? What about when I changed into the blob on Kippo VI and saved everybody? Whose idea was that?"*

"Actually, it was mine. When I briefed you last time, I left subliminal messages that prompted your symbiote to transform itself into an Algolian blob. A touch of genius, if I do say so myself." Tracer's smug voice suddenly became irritated. *"Who would have thought that a small, insignificant planet like Helios would have the protection of a Chain? It certainly wasn't authorized by the FOEs. Not unless The Tyrant gave the order himself."*

Loaf was still feeling defiant. *"Why don't you ask him?"*

There was an edge to Tracer's voice. *"Don't get cute, Earthling. Nobody questions The Tyrant."* The voice in Loaf's head became smug once more. *"It doesn't matter. Your signal is on the move, so you must have found alternative transportation. A spaceship, I presume."*

"Yeah," said Loaf grudgingly. *"We got a lift with some guy called Hobo."*

"And you still have The Server?"

"Yeah."

"Good. Well, bon voyage. Next stop, He-lios — and don't worry, I'll be with you all the way. Now forget everything we've just said and keep on going!" Tracer cooed. *"Lead me to The Server and The Weaver!"*

Loaf moaned in his sleep.

Beep-beeeep-beep! Beeeep-beep-beeeep! Beep-beeeep-beep!

A series of shrill alarms pierced the still-ness of the cabin. Loaf leaped up and cracked his head on an instrument panel. Bitz yapped. "Wassup? Wassup?!"

"What's the pitch now, *Trigger*?" asked Zo-diac.

"It seems that we've picked up a distress signal," the ship answered.

The beeps continued to shriek out in a dis-cernible pattern.

"It's like a series of dots and dashes," said Merle.

Zodiac nodded. "You're right, dudette. It's Coarse code — primitive, but effective in an emergency. We've got ourselves a 'please-help-our-butts-we're-out-of-the-air-lock-with-out-a-space-suit' Me-day call."

"Don't you mean a Mayday call?" asked Jack.

"No, dude. 'Me, me, me.' In an emergency, it's every being for itself."

Bitz gave a yelp. "Has this tub got an emergency frequency viewscreen?"

Zodiac looked hurt. "Sure thing. Hey, *Trigger*! You want to activate the viewscreen?" There was a pause while nothing happened. "Please?"

"Well, since you ask so nicely," *Trigger* said in prim tones. "Good manners cost nothing and they'll get you a long way."

A viewscreen unfolded from the ceiling.

Merle gasped. A group of six or seven female humanoid faces peered out. They had blue skin and matted green hair, which hung loose. All of the faces were gaunt. The picture pulled back to reveal several smaller figures sitting and lying on the floor. Behind the group, Jack could just make out what he presumed to be the badly damaged control deck of a spaceship.

"Women and children," said Bitz. "And they look like they're in trouble."

One of the humanoid creatures opened its mouth. The most incredible sound poured from the ship's speakers. Jack was transfixed by the beauty of the voice. It was not speech; it was more like music, but not the jangling, repetitive sound of a pop song. The voice seemed to be delivered on several pitches at once, harmonizing with itself. The melody rose and fell, swirling around the cabin, full of fear, hope, and yearning. Without a doubt, it was the most beautiful voice Jack had ever heard. The hairs on the back of his neck stood on end, and he shivered as the sound swept through his body, touching his very core.

The Server's translation application, having analyzed the unknown language, cut in. Jack, Loaf, and Merle could now understand the urgent message contained in the song.

"My name is Molpe. My people are from the planet Ligeia. We are refugees, trying to escape persecution from the FOEs regime on our planet. We are few in number but brave in spirit. During our escape, we were fired upon, and our power source has been damaged.

We are marooned, and our life-support systems are failing. We have little time. Help us.
Please."

The others took up the pleading, their
voices joining the first like a great, soaring
chorus. "Help us, please. Please, please . . ."

CHAPTER SEVEN

"Where's this message coming from?" asked Googie.

"Any ideas, *Trigger*?" asked Zodiac as politely as he could.

Trigger gave a sigh. "Of course I know. It is being transmitted from a ship in the adjoining sector."

"And how far away is it?" asked Jack.

"I could reach it in two point one-three Gala-hours at whoosh factor five. Or in one point two Gala-hours at whoosh factor eight, which I don't recommend, as *someone* hasn't bothered tuning up my engines for quite a while. Incidentally, there is no other ship that could answer the distress call. I am the nearest vessel."

"Thank you," said Jack. He turned to face the viewscreen. The chorus of pleading continued to wash around the cabin interior.

Zodiac held out his orange hands, palms up. "So what's the plan, space rangers?"

"We help them, of course," said Jack.

Merle shook her head in disagreement. "We don't have a clue who or what those things are. It could be a trap."

"She's right," agreed Googie. "This is a classic FOEs trick. They're bait. They're the cheese, we're the mice. They lure us there and *SNAP* — the trap springs shut!"

Bitz nodded. "I hate to agree with the cat, but we should be careful. We have to think of our mission."

Everyone looked toward Loaf, who gave a dismissive shrug. "Why bother? It's not our problem. Let them stew."

Jack breathed deeply. "We have to rescue them. You heard what they said: They're dying. All of them. What if it was us in danger?"

"But it isn't," Loaf pointed out. "Let's keep it that way."

Jack glared at him.

Merle looked uncomfortable. "We could come back and rescue them after we've been to Helios."

"How long will that take?" snapped Jack. "Can we really save the Galaxy from evil by letting innocent people die? If we do nothing, the FOEs win!"

Merle looked down to avoid Jack's stare.

Zodiac sniffed and wiped a tear from his eye. "That's beautiful, dude, just beautiful. You sure have a way with words. Like they say, 'A friend in need is a friend indeed.'"

"A friend in need is a pain in the butt," meowed Googie. "I stick by what I said — it's a trap." Bitz nodded in agreement.

Jack stood up. "Janus gave me the responsibility for this mission. We go to Helios and find the sightless one . . ."

Merle gave a sigh of relief. It was short-lived.

". . . after we've rescued the people on that ship!"

Merle shook her head, and Googie gave a disgusted meow.

Bitz growled. "Okay, Jack. If you think we should do this, we'll do it . . ."

"Thanks, Bitz," said Jack, relieved to have found some support.

" . . . even if you are wrong."

Nobody spoke during the journey to the stricken spaceship. The crew of *Trigger* sat grim-faced. Above them, the faces of Molpe and her people continued their pleas. The urgent music of their appeal for help echoed through the cabin, urging them on, drawing them ever closer.

After two Gala-hours of traveling at whoosh factor five, *Trigger* began to slow down. "Stranded vessel in range."

Six faces peered out the window into the blackness.

"There she rolls!" cried Zodiac.

The others turned quickly to where he was pointing. A short distance away, to the starboard of *Trigger*, was a wheel-shaped vessel, slowly rotating on its axis.

"So what do we do now?" asked Loaf. But before anyone could answer, *Trigger* gave a huge lurch and began to pitch wildly. Jack, Merle, Loaf, and Zodiac fell back into their seats with bruising thumps. Googie and Bitz flew across the floor and crashed into the hard metallic wall.

"OW! OOH! EEK!" cried *Trigger* as it bounced up and down.

"Solar wind!" yelled Zodiac. "Where in the great Galaxy did that come from?" He was cut off as another gust buffeted *Trigger*, spinning the ship around as if it were a leaf in a windstorm.

A loud screeching blared out from the speakers. Jack glanced up at the viewscreen and his stomach turned. The humanoid forms they had come to rescue had been replaced by jellylike blobs. Shimmering blue skins had metamorphosed into ugly, pockmarked, decomposing faces. Reptilian tongues and vicious fangs protruded from slobbering mouths.

The beautiful voices were now discordant shrieks and howls. "Come to us! To your doom!"

"This is heavy-duty," moaned Zodiac. "As they say, 'We're up a black hole without retro rockets.'"

"This is another fine mess you've gotten me into," screamed *Trigger*. "Trust you to bring us into the middle of a meteor storm."

"What meteors?" Merle's voice quaked.

"Those meteors!" Zodiac grimaced and motioned with his head. "*Trigger*'s right — we've got galactic garden rockery heading straight toward us. Man, what a bummer!"

In the distance, moving at incredible speed, was a swarm of meteors. It was spread out across the blackness as far as the eye could see. Hundreds upon hundreds of rocks of all shapes and sizes hurtled toward *Trigger* and its occupants.

Googie gave a yowl. "I know that it's not the time to say I told you so, but I want it on record that I told you so."

The group stared helplessly at the incoming storm of destruction. As *Trigger* rocked from side to side, the faces on the viewscreen leered with hatred, and the speakers crackled with the wails and squawks of the diabolical creatures who had lured them to their doom. "Haaaaaaaaa! To your doom! To your doom!"

"I can't avoid them all." *Trigger* sounded panicked. "There are too many."

"TRY!" screamed everyone.

"Now you're *all* shouting at me. . . ." *Trigger* burst into tears.

"Oh, dude, we are goners," moaned Zodiac. "We can't go around it, we can't go over it, we can't go under it. We'll have to go through it and get smashed to a pulp!"

Merle glared at him. "What's the matter with you? You're supposed to be a pilot. Switch to manual and fly through them."

Zodiac gave her an appalled stare. "Me? Fly? I don't do that Captain Space-hero stuff! I just tell the ship what to do and it does it! Sometimes," he added ruefully.

Loaf glared at him, wide-eyed with fury. "Are you telling me you can't even fly? Does this rust bucket have manual controls?"

"Somewhere, I guess . . ."

Merle pointed. "Try that button there. The one that says MANUAL CONTROL."

Zodiac stared at the button as if he'd never seen it before. "Hey, wild!" He pressed it, and a section of the control panel opened in front of him. A joystick appeared.

Loaf's eyes lit up. He shoved Zodiac out of the pilot's seat and took his place. "Now that's what I'm talking about!"

Ignoring startled protests from Bitz and Merle, Loaf grabbed the joystick and waggled it experimentally. *Trigger* swooped in a wild spiral.

"Stop it! You're making me nauseous!"

"Loaf," protested Merle, "you don't know how to fly a spaceship!"

Loaf didn't take his eyes off the approaching meteors. "What's to know? It's just like Asteroid Crash II. All you have to do is fly between the rocks, and I happen to hold the all-time record on the snack bar machine back on the base. Relax and watch an expert in action." He maneuvered *Trigger* to face the oncoming rocks.

Jack gave a helpless shrug. "All right. Just remember, in this game you've only got one life — and so do the rest of us!"

Zodiac moaned and held his head in his hands. "Here we go! Whoosh factor three and fear factor ten."

Trigger shot toward the meteors, the meteors shot toward *Trigger*. Screams shot around the cabin.

Jack shook his head in apology. "I know it's a bad time to say I'm sorry I got you all into this, but I'm sorry."

"Put it on your tombstone," growled Googie.

Trigger was being rocked from side to side

as the wind jarred and jolted the craft. Zodiac could be heard muttering under his breath, "Be cool, be cool. Chill, relax. Fear is an illusion. Think positive thoughts, and all will be well."

BOOOF! A rock bounced off *Trigger's* hull.

"Ow! That hurt!" the ship wailed.

Loaf immediately executed a series of bone-jarring twists and spins in an effort to avoid the oncoming meteors. "Waaaaaaaa!" he yelled in exhilaration.

"Waaaaaaaaaaaaaa!" screamed the others in terror.

The rocks kept coming, wave upon wave of them. Loaf flung *Trigger* from side to side and even upside down in his attempts to avoid crashing into them. Jack stared wide-eyed at the projectiles of death as they flashed by. It was like an arcade game played in triple time.

Googie and Bitz were hanging on by the skin of their teeth. Quite literally. Bitz had his jaws clamped firmly into a metal chair leg. "Thith ith goin koo ruin gy keeth." He grimaced as he flipped up and down like a fish on the end of a line.

Merle gave a howl of pain. "Will you get your claws out of my neck?"

122

Googie tightened her grip. "Sorry, human. Any port in a meteor storm. Wear a scarf next time."

Still the rocks came. Still Loaf managed to dodge them. *Trigger*'s panic-stricken voice provided a running commentary. "What are you doing? Watch out for that rock. Be careful. Left, right, oh, no!"

"Lay off the backseat driving," Loaf muttered.

Several voices chorused, "Heeeeellllp!"

Ching! The hologram appeared from The Server, wearing a nightcap. He yawned. "Hey, I was sound asleep, what's the . . ." Help glanced at the torrent of rocks whizzing by the window and did a double take. "Holy . . ." He disappeared back into The Server. A sign appeared over the HELP button:

TheRe iS No oNE aVailaBLe To TaKe yoUr CaLL. PLeaSe sCreaM aFteR the toNe.

The maelstrom continued. The gloating of the foul beings that had lured them into the path of the deadly storm changed to shrieks of rage. These were punctuated by metallic clangs that echoed around the cabin as Loaf failed to dodge some of the smaller meteors. How long it lasted was impossible to say; time seemed to stand still, zoom along, slow down, and speed up again all at once. Everything was a blur of rocks and light.

And suddenly, it was over. Space cleared before them and became, once again, a peaceful, vast, twinkling cosmos.

Loaf punched the air. "Whoooeee! Top score! I am the Man!"

Bitz let go of the chair leg and dropped to the floor with a thump. "Gy jaw is thut tholid."

Jack looked toward the viewscreen. It was blank — the creatures that sought their destruction had disappeared. He turned to the others. "Sorry. I should have listened," he said sheepishly.

"You were concerned," said Merle, rubbing at her wrists and arms in an attempt to get her blood circulating again. "That's a good thing. Even if it did nearly get us smashed to bits."

Googie gave a hiss. "Humans — far too caring and sentimental."

"*I* said we should've left them alone," interjected Loaf.

Googie looked at Loaf. "I suppose every species has its exceptions."

"Hey, who just saved your sorry hides — *again*?" demanded Loaf. "Cut the wise-cracks!"

Jack patted Loaf on the shoulder. "Yeah. Thanks."

"Who were those creeps?" asked Merle. "FOEs?"

"I don't think so," replied Googie. "The FOEs wouldn't have wanted to destroy us — they want The Server in one piece. That was local action. The Galaxy's full of space pirates and such. They lie in wait and lure unsuspecting ships into meteor storms and then pick up the pieces afterward."

"The cat's right," drawled Zodiac. He patted the control console. "Hey, *Trigger*, did you dig that flying? Pretty fancy stuff, huh?"

"I could have done just as well," replied the ship, "if not better. . . ."

Zodiac gave a big sigh. "Well, rock riders, I'm all pooped out after that adrenaline rush. Whaddaya say we all take a big time-out?" He pointed toward a large asteroid that floated in the distance. "Set us down there, *Trigger*. We'll do a damage check and get our bearings."

Within minutes, *Trigger* was closing in on the pale-colored, crater-pocked surface. "Hold tight for landing procedures. Please fasten your seat belts, fold up your tray tables, and make sure your seats are in the upright position."

Jack looked down toward the looming surface and gave a gasp of horror. He blinked, shook his head, and stared again. There was a movement from the surface. No, that wasn't right. Not *from* the surface: The *whole* surface was moving.

"Er . . . Zodiac, what are asteroids made from?"

"Rock, metal ores, that kind of thing."

Jack looked again. After his last blunder, he was unsure whether to voice his concerns. "Do asteroids have eyes that blink?"

"Whooa dude. You've been in space too long. No way."

"And I suppose if I said that an asteroid was trying to grab us, you'd say it was just my imagination?"

The cabin rocked as huge tentacles began to wrap themselves around *Trigger*. The "asteroid" unfolded, revealing itself to be a giant floating space creature. Its seven eyes stared at the ship, and more tentacles reached forward to grasp its prey.

"It's a silla!" yapped Bitz. "They trap spaceships, crush them, and eat them!"

"Stop tickling! Stop it, stop it, stop it!" cried *Trigger* as the silla's tentacles tightened.

"Use your weapons!" cried Googie.

"Ermmm. No can do," Zodiac said in a resigned way.

"Are you telling me that this ship doesn't have any defense system of any kind?" yelled Googie.

"Sorry, cat. This is a purely peace-loving vessel."

"*We'll* be in pieces if those tentacles get any tighter!"

"Why is the Galaxy full of creatures that want to do nasty things to us?" complained Merle.

More tentacles curled themselves around *Trigger*'s hull.

"It's stopped tickling! Now it's crushing me! Oooo! Help!"

Help materialized. "Have the rocks gone?"

Jack nodded, "Yes, but they've been replaced by that."

The hologram stared wide-eyed as a tentacle slithered across the window. "Bye . . ." Help vanished. A new sign appeared:

> *The application you requested*
> *has not been recognized.*
> *KluDge oFF!*

"What sort of Help are you?" called Merle. "Are you a hologram or a mouse?"

A third sign appeared:

> *SqUeaK!*

Zodiac tapped maniacally at the console. "Come on, *Trigger*, honey, give me full power, rev it up. Come on, sweet thing! Hit reverse."

The ship obeyed but was unable to pull free from the silla's deadly grip.

"I can't!" sobbed *Trigger*. "I'm just useless!"

"No, you're not," Zodiac reassured it. He

gestured to the others, who took his hint and joined in the encouragement.

"Come on! You can do it."

Trigger's efforts were proving futile. Its hull began to groan under the pressure. Small cracks appeared in its plating.

Merle suddenly snapped her fingers. "Change direction!" she ordered. "Go forward! Full power."

Zodiac looked puzzled. "Forward? *At* the big, wriggly dude?"

"Yes. Now!"

Trigger obeyed.

The silla wasn't expecting such a sudden change in direction. Its grip on *Trigger* loosened. The ship catapulted forward and flew headlong into one of the silla's eyes. The creature's tentacles unraveled.

"Free!" *Trigger* quickly reversed, before shooting forward in a tight turn that took it back over the creature's flapping appendages. The craft did a little celebratory roll as it sped away from the massive predator.

Jack whooped with relief. "Nice going, Merle."

"I did it on my unarmed combat course," said Merle happily. "First rule of self-defense — if someone's attacking you, go for their weakest point."

The ship continued to shoot through space at full tilt.

"Hey, *Trigger*, dude, we're out of there," said Zodiac. "No need to be traveling at whoosh factor five . . . six . . . seven. . . ." His expression changed to one of alarm. "Hey, slow down, hot rod . . . eight . . . nine . . . cool it!! . . . ten . . . eleven . . . eleven?! You can't go this fast!"

"I can't slow down!" wailed the ship. "I'm being pulled along."

Merle looked outside. Light seemed to be overtaking the ship. "If we're going forward, shouldn't the light be coming toward us, not passing us from behind?"

"Oh, man!" Zodiac pointed a quivering finger. "What a downer! This is the cosmic pits. . . ."

Before them was a sphere of total blackness. Light swirled around its periphery like water around a drain before being pulled into the mighty depths of the most lethal phenomenon in the universe — a black hole.

"We're trapped!" screeched Loaf. "It's pulling us in."

The awesome power of the black hole was too much for the efforts of the ship. Jack and the others stared in horror as the region of utter darkness expanded to fill their vision.

"When do we hit event horizon?" yelled Googie.

"What's that?" asked Loaf.

"The point of no return. The moment when nothing can escape from the pull of the blaaack hoooooole."

"Toooo laaate, weeee've alreeeeady hiiiiiiit iiiiiiiiit." *Trigger* groaned. "Ohhhhhhhhhhh, myyyyyyyyyyyyyyyyyyyyyyyy!"

Trigger's voice slowed as the black hole warped time and space. Inside the cabin, other interesting changes were taking place. Loaf was the first to notice. His feet were being stretched out, as if he were on a rack. His legs followed suit. He turned, panic-stricken, to the others. They were in the same predicament, their bodies stretched out as if in a fun-house mirror.

"Whaaaaaaat's haaaaaaappeniiiiiiiiiiiiing?" moaned Loaf.

"Weeee're spaaaaghetiiiifyyyyyying," rumbled Merle.

"Heeeellllppp," howled Loaf. "I dooon'ttt waaaant toooo beee aaa noooooodle . . ."

Their bodies continued to stretch in the pull of an enormous gravity field. Jack and his companions were becoming very thin, very quickly. Loaf looked like the world's tallest basketball player, and Bitz had turned into an elongated dachshund.

Jack felt numb with despair. After all the dangers they had faced, their quest was about to end here as their bodies were torn apart, molecule by molecule, in the irresistible vortex of the black hole.

CHAPTER EIGHT

Amid the distorted chaos of the black hole's effects, The Server alone retained its square shape. Jack grabbed at this life-line.

"Heeeeeeeeeellllllllllllllppppppppppppppp!" Jack's despairing cry echoed around the stretched-out cabin of the doomed ship.

The hologram appeared. "I take it you've escaped from the tentacle thing. Good! So what's wrong now? We heading for a black hole or somethin'? Haa-haa, ha-h —" Help's laugh died away as it took in the living spaghetti all around the cabin. "Hit t-mail!" it shrieked. "Now!"

Jack's sixty-foot-long finger, moving with the speed of a slow-motion replay of a snail race, hit the TELEPORT key.

There was an explosion of light, a rush of air, and then silence.

Molecules rearranged themselves into their normal combinations as ship and crew reappeared some distance from the grip of the black hole.

"Starboard turn, full power!" ordered Help. "Get out of here!"

The ship responded immediately. Within the blink of an electromagnetic pulse, *Trigger* once again pulled away from danger.

Everyone fell back and panted with relief.

Help materialized a trumpet and blew a tinny fanfare. Clouds of virtual ticker tape swirled around his holographic head. Ain't I the best!"

"How did you get us out of there?" asked Merle.

"Easy PC!" trilled Help. "I programmed The Server to t-mail the ship and occupants back into open space, beyond the pull of the black hole!"

"You can do that?" asked Jack. "T-mail to any point in space?"

"I just did, didn't I? I don't usually do it, though, because what's the point? You've seen one cubic kilometer of space, you've seen 'em all."

Jack wagged his finger in the smirking hologram's face. "You could have t-mailed us out of the meteor storm or out of the silla's grip?"

"Sure, I could," agreed Help brightly. "But if I helped you out of every jam, what would you do for excitement? Let's have less of this third-degree stuff! Didn't I just save your sorry butts? Huh, primates! That's gratitude for ya!" The hologram shot back into The Server.

"Let's get to Helios," said Googie wearily. "I'm running out of lives."

Temple of the Five Winds, Planet Helios, Trojan Sector

Forty-eight Gala-hours later, *Trigger*'s air lock cracked open. The disembarkation ramp swung jerkily into position. Jack stepped out into the air of Helios. Instantly, a half-dozen begging bowls were thrust under his nose.

"Fates bless you, young Master. Please give generously to the *Way of Kerching*."

"Hey, chill, you guys!" Zodiac pushed his

way amiably through the small crowd of Collectors that had gathered in the brief minutes since the ship had touched down. "Don't hassle us, we only just got here." The pilot spread his arms wide as if he had personally created the entire planet and arranged everything on it for his passengers' gratification. "Welcome to Helios!"

Since their escape from the black hole, the trip to Helios had been uneventful. Even *Trigger* had become more communicative, though the ship's brain had developed a tendency to have private whispered conversations with Help that involved a lot of snickering, giving their organic shipmates an uncomfortable feeling of being laughed at.

Jack had insisted on spending time during the trip studying their destination. The FIB files on Helios had described the group of the Collectors. Jack and his companions had identified the Temple of the Five Winds as being a likely place to start their search for the "sightless one who sees all things," as Janus had cryptically described the guide who might lead them to The Weaver. And so, Zodiac had brought them to a not so smooth landing in a clearing between gnarled and stunted trees within walking distance of the temple.

Jack stepped off the ramp, taking in the warm, scented air, the sounds of alien insect life, and the warmth of the three Helian suns. He gazed at the sky that was a deeper blue than Earth's, cloudless and tinged with green where it met the horizon. His glance rested on the Collectors, whose leathery faces were set in professionally friendly grins.

"We're looking for a prophet," he said hesitantly.

Instantly, the bowls were thrust under his nose again. "So are we!"

"Jeepers!" The Server's translator program was working overtime as it converted Bitz's growls simultaneously into English for Merle, Jack, and Loaf, Kippan for Googie, Jivan for Zodiac, and Helian for the Collectors. "He doesn't mean p-r-o-f-i-t! He means p-r-o-p-h-e-t as in sage, seer, or shaman. You know, Wise Being of the Mountain. Lord High Muckety-muck or panjandrum. Whatever."

The foremost of the Collectors brightened. "Ah! You seek enlightenment?"

"I guess. . . ." said Merle uncertainly.

The Collector gestured with his bowl. "Please follow. We will take you to the Master Collector."

Jack stepped forward. An odd little procession formed. The Collector led the way. He was followed by Jack, carrying the Server. Bitz trotted at his heels. After them came Merle, carrying Googie, and Loaf, who was slouching with his hands in his pockets. A small crowd of Collectors, their robes hitched to knee height, formed lines on each side of them, chattering excitedly and occasionally holding out their bowls, more in hope than anticipation. The ambling figure of Zodiac brought up the rear.

The companions approached the Temple of the Five Winds, from which the solemn chants of the afternoon devotions wavered on the soft breeze.

"Pm . . . pm . . . pm . . ."

The Master awaited them in the great hall of the temple. He bowed deeply. "Greetings, travelers from many far-off worlds. Welcome to the Temple of the Five Winds. I understand that you have come here seeking enlightenment."

"Maybe," said Loaf suspiciously. "What does it cost?" Jack kicked him in the shin.

The Master smiled the smile of one who has studied long to perfect the Ancient Art of Ignoring Stupid Remarks. "Here you may learn much. And perhaps we may learn much from all of you."

Merle gave Loaf a sour look. "I wouldn't count on it."

"We have been expecting you," said the Master calmly. "Your coming was predicted many days ago by the sightless one who sees all things."

Jack gave a start. He exchanged an astonished glance with Merle, then turned back to the Master, keeping his voice level with an effort. "Yes. That is who we have come to see."

"So, you wish to see Tiresias?" The Master's face was impassive.

"If Tiresias is the sightless one who sees all things," said Jack firmly, "our mission is to find and ask him to guide us on our way."

"I see." The Master Collector bowed his head in thought. "We are simple Collectors, we who follow the *Way of Kerching*. We seek only enlightenment. And donations." He whipped a begging bowl from his sleeve and held it out hopefully. His visitors ignored it. The Master sighed and replaced the bowl in his sleeve. "Sorry. Force of habit.

"Tiresias requires silence and tranquillity to meditate. Your visit must be brief, and you must not disturb the sightless one. You must not press Tiresias to give answers to your questions. Only one of you must speak." The Master held up a hand to forestall protests. "The sightless one is a being apart. These are our conditions."

Jack looked questioningly at the others. Merle nodded. Loaf shrugged. Bitz had his head on one side, considering. Googie, grooming her ears, failed to meet Jack's eye, as did Zodiac who appeared to have gone to sleep standing up.

"All right," Jack told the Master. "We accept your conditions. We will come with you to see Tiresias."

The Master nodded. "You will also bring the . . . machine you carry. It will . . . interest Tiresias."

For a moment, Jack caught a glimpse of

something other than impassive serenity in the Master's eyes. He thought he detected anxiety — and greed. Then the moment passed. The Master stood before him, benign and serene. Jack shrugged. "All right," he said again.

The Master bowed and turned away. Jack beckoned to the others and followed.

Zodiac woke with a start. "Where we goin'?"

Merle grinned. "Just to see some guy. Are you coming?"

Zodiac shrugged. "I guess."

They followed the Master out of the candlelit hall, down a corridor lit by flickering lamps. They passed through a wooden door, down a ramp, and along another corridor whose straight stone walls looked smoother than those of the higher passageway. It was lit by hissing globes that looked as if they were fueled by gas.

Next came a bronze door, another ramp, and a corridor whose walls were seamless and smooth as marble, shining in the light of electric lamps. Jack was puzzled. It was as if their journey down into the depths of the temple was also a journey forward through time. He glanced at Merle, who nodded and shrugged. She had noticed the oddness of their surroundings, too – but there was no time for discussion.

The Master paused before a steel door and pressed his hand to a flat plate set into the wall beside it. The plate glowed. Jack frowned. A palm-print reader! That was a pretty snazzy locking mechanism for a bunch of reclusive Collectors whose only interests were enlightenment and handouts. Jack felt the hairs on the back of his neck begin to rise. At his feet, Bitz growled deep in his throat.

The door slid aside. The Master stepped through into a long chamber.

The lighting was subdued. The walls, floor, and ceiling were made of some semitransparent material that Jack could not identify, which pulsed with bars and points of light. A low hum filled the chamber. Jack had the impression that if he could only hear it properly, the noise would prove to be a billion noises of different frequencies and pitches, all combined into one indistinct sound.

Overlying the background noise was the monotonous chanting of the dozen or so gray-clad Collectors who knelt at intervals along both sides of the chamber, totally muffled in their novices' robes. "Sum . . . sum . . . sum . . ."

In the center of the chamber, a figure sat on a plain wooden chair. It wore gray vestments. Its arms were hidden by voluminous sleeves. The shape of its body was lost within its formless habit, and its hood was pulled so far forward that nothing of its face was visible.

The Master stood aside to allow the visitors to approach the still figure.

Slowly, Jack stepped forward. He held The Server in arms folded against his chest. His throat was dry as he looked vainly up into the shadows of the hood.

"Are you Tiresias?"

The figure stirred. In a voice that sounded like the creaking of some mechanism long unused, it said, "I am."

"And the sightless one who sees all things?"

"So am I known to some."

Jack looked back to Merle, who gave him a nod of encouragement, and Bitz, who still had his head to one side and his eyes narrowed in an expression of uncertainty. Jack turned back to face the being called Tiresias.

"We are Friends of the Outernet," he said, choosing his words carefully. "We are searching for The Weaver. We received a message from Agent Janus."

There was a sharp intake of breath from the shadowy figure. "But Janus is dead. He fell into N-space, from which there is no return."

Jack heard Bitz growl softly behind him. "How does he know that?"

Tiresias said a little quickly, "I am the sightless one who sees all things."

"Oh, yeah," said Bitz in a suspicious voice. "I forgot."

"Only one must speak," the Master reminded them, with a pointed glare at the dog.

Jack continued, "Janus is still alive, somehow. He contacted us from N-space. He told us to seek you. He said you had information about where we could find The Weaver. Is that true?"

Tiresias nodded. "It is. I see you have an Outernet server with you." The cloaked figure extended a wrinkled claw from one of its sleeves and pointed to its knees. "Bring it to me. I shall enter the coordinates of The Weaver's position so that you may teleport directly to your goal." For a moment, Jack thought he saw a flash of light deep within the hood, then it was gone.

Jack hesitated — and slowly stepped forward.

Bitz shook his head. "This isn't right." He gave an uneasy whine. "It can't be this easy."

"Don't knock it," said Loaf. "I like easy."

Zodiac nodded in agreement. "Amen to that, dude. Easy is cool."

But Googie was also apprehensive. Her tail twitched. "There's something wrong." With narrowed eyes, she watched the chanting Collectors lining the walls.

"You bet there's something wrong!" Bitz was growling now. "What about the Chain around this planet? Who put it there? And how can we teleport to where The Weaver is with the Chain in place?" Bitz leaped to his feet. "Jack, wait!"

Jack, who had been about to place The Server on Tiresias's cloaked lap, hesitated.

"Do not be concerned." There was an edge

to Tiresias's voice now. "Give me The Server."
A wrinkled, mottled claw reached out. Jack
snatched The Server back and stared at the
claw with disquiet. Where had he seen it before?

At the same moment, Googie leaped,
snarling and spitting, at the nearest Collector.
The cat's unexpected assault caused the Collector to pull back in alarm. Something bright
fell from his robes and landed on the floor
with a clatter. The Collectors stopped chanting. Every eye in the room shot toward the
sound and focused on the deadly looking energy weapon that had been concealed under
the Collector's habit.

Googie patted at it with a cautious forepaw.
"Well," she drawled, looking up into the Collector's cowl. "That doesn't look very enlightened to *me*."

Merle was the first to recover from the moment of stillness following this discovery. She
leaped forward and grabbed the weapon before anyone else could move and pointed it
rather shakily at the figure of Tiresias. "I've got
you covered. Don't move!"

"Actually, you're pointing that weapon the wrong way." Tiresias's voice had risen several octaves from its bass growl and now sounded light and almost jovial.

Hurriedly, Merle swung the energy weapon around. "Is that better?"

"Much better. Now, if you can only find the safety catch. . . ."

Merle gestured threateningly with the weapon. "Don't try messing with me. Hands up!"

"Certainly." Tiresias stood and raised his arms — all six of them. At the same moment, the Collectors lining the walls lumbered to their feet and threw off their robes, revealing themselves as Bugs. They all raised hidden weapons, menacing the humans and their companions.

"Hey!" Loaf's cry was outraged. "This is a setup!"

"Well, it took you long enough to spot it!" Tiresias spoke in an amused manner. "Why don't you just hand over The Server and save yourselves an infinity of pain?"

Tiresias reached up with four of its claws

and pulled back its hood to reveal a familiar elephant-eared head. His mouth was pinched, and where his eyes should have been was a VR visor.

Jack gripped The Server more tightly and stared at the unveiled figure in horror and dismay. "Tracer!"

CHAPTER NINE

Jack glared at The Tyrant's communications officer. "How did you know where to find us?"

Tracer gave an amused chuckle. "It wasn't so hard. I've been following your progress since Deadrock. I left Kazamblam as soon as your friend here told me where you were headed." He waved a negligent claw toward where Loaf was standing.

"I knew it!" Merle pointed an accusing finger at Loaf. "You traitor!"

Loaf was thunderstruck. "I never told him anything!"

"Don't give me that!" Merle was beside herself with fury. Bitz growled and Googie flattened her ears and spat at Loaf. "You *were* reformatted on Deadrock. I knew it!"

"You do your friend an injustice," said

Tracer cheerfully, "difficult though that might be. He was not reformatted — it was unnecessary, because we found him to be as sneaky, self-obsessed, and devious as even The Tyrant could desire."

"Hey!" protested Loaf.

"On the other hand, we did implant a tracking device in the base of what I suppose we must laughingly call his brain, and I have been in touch with him several times, using the atrocious MindMelt technique."

"He's lying!" howled Loaf. "What MindMelt technique? Aaaaaaarrrggghh!"

"*That* MindMelt technique," said Tracer as Loaf rolled around on the floor, clutching at his head. "I contacted him in his sleep and ordered him to forget that I had done so. I used him to follow you — but I can't take any credit for instances of cowardice, selfishness, or duplicity committed by your friend on the way here. Far from being prompted by me, any such despicable acts were merely the results of his charmless and egotistical personality."

Merle gave the moaning Loaf an angry glare, then she lifted her energy weapon and squared her shoulders. "Okay, gang," she cried in ringing tones, "let's get 'em!"

The others stared at her.

"Merle," said Jack, unhappily eyeing the opposition, "I'm not sure that's wise."

"Are you out of your *mind*?" demanded Googie. "I hate to be a killjoy, but there are a dozen highly trained Bugs in here with big energy weapons and bad tempers. There are only five of us, and you're the only one who's armed."

"Six," corrected Merle. "Zodiac's with us, aren't you, Zodiac?"

Zodiac looked alarmed. "Hey, dudette, no way! I'm strictly a noncombatant. I've dodged so many drafts, people hire me to check their air-conditioning."

"Now listen to me, Zodiac!" snapped Merle, her eyes flashing. "Don't justice, freedom, and honor mean anything to you? You can walk away from us right now if you want. But then you'll spend the rest of your life knowing you had the chance to change history, and you blew it. Can you live with that?" Merle's voice rang through the still air in challenge. "Go ahead! Show us that you really are just a no-account space bum after all, and that's all you'll ever be!"

Zodiac shrugged. "Guess you're right." He turned to Tracer. "Can I go now?"

Tracer gestured expansively. "Oh, I guess so, Mr. Hobo. Just don't do anything to annoy The Tyrant."

"You got it, big guy." Zodiac shuffled toward the door.

Merle was stunned. "Hey! You can't do this! This isn't how it happens in the movies! You're supposed to be shamed into helping us defeat the bad guys."

Zodiac looked back briefly and shrugged. "Too many bad guys, not enough shame. Sorry, dudette. See you around. . . ." Zodiac looked at the heavily armed Bugs. "On the other hand, I guess I won't. Nice to meet you folks, it's been a blast." He eyed the Bugs' powerful energy weapons, poised and ready to fire. "Oops. Poor choice of words. You know what I mean." The door slammed shut.

Merle seethed with anger for a moment, then switched her attack to the Master Collector. "And as for you! Some enlightened Master you turned out to be. You led us into a trap!"

The Master's face remained inscrutable. "Your struggle is not our struggle. We have tried to keep outsiders away by setting up a Chain to deter t-mail incursions, but, nevertheless, you have found your way here and must bear the consequences. We do not wish to be involved. When the FOEs arrived, they threatened to destroy Tiresias if we did not cooperate. We had no alternative."

"Ha!" Merle's shoulders slumped. She dropped the energy weapon and turned to Jack. "Like you said, evil triumphs if good people do nothing."

"Just a minute." Jack's mind was racing. He stared at the Master. "You said the FOEs threatened to destroy Tiresias." Jack pointed at Tracer. "Obviously, *that* isn't the real Tiresias. But I can't believe that Janus would have misled us. So who — or what — *is* Tiresias?"

Tracer grinned. "Show them," he said.

The Master looked startled. "Honored Lord . . ."

"Show them, I said. I see no reason not to satisfy their curiosity." Tracer nodded to Jack. "Bring The Server."

The Master bowed to Tracer and turned to the companions. "This room is merely one aspect of Tiresias. Come." He stepped past Tracer, who fell into step behind him, and beckoned Jack and his companions to follow with a cheery wave. The Bugs fell in on either side, on the alert for any trouble.

At the far end of the room was a circular opening in the floor. Jack guessed what it was even before the Master, with studied unconcern, stepped into it and dropped from sight. An antigravity lift! Jack hesitated — and one of the Bugs motioned him forward with his weapon. Jack steeled himself, grasped The Server tightly, and walked out onto thin air.

The descent was slower than a free fall but fast enough to be uncomfortable. Jack and Merle tumbled helplessly; Loaf, spinning above them, howled with fright. The others, used to this method of travel, dropped in a more controlled way, occasionally correcting their position with motions of their hands and feet — or paws in the case of Googie and Bitz.

Merle groaned. "I feel like Alice in Wonderland," she muttered. "I wonder if we'll find a white rabbit at the bottom." Jack, still clutching The Server, watched the smooth sides of the shaft fly by and said nothing.

Eventually, their descent slowed. Weight returned, and the humans fought to regain an upright position before landing with a gentle bump on a smooth floor. The Master waited until Jack and Merle had helped Loaf (who had landed on his head) and then led the party toward a wide opening beyond which they glimpsed the rocky walls of a vast cavern. They stepped through the opening onto a ledge furnished with control consoles, several of which were manned by Collectors, and protected by a simple metal handrail.

The Master indicated that they should look over the edge. "Behold Tiresias!"

Merle stepped back and put her hand over her mouth. Loaf gave a horrified moan. Bitz shrunk back and whined. Googie spat. Tracer, watching their reactions, chuckled. The Bugs stood impassively at attention.

Only Jack, though every nerve in his body shrieked at him to get away, remained at the

155

rail, staring down at the monstrous sight below.

A huge, quivering, bloated mass of transparent flesh heaved disgustingly beneath the ledge. The horrendous creature that lay helpless in the cavern below looked like a cross between a decomposing octopus and a diseased jellyfish. Garish, iridescent flashes of color seethed through its body like sheet lightning. Around the cavern, ten colossal tentaclelike limbs climbed the rocky walls to disappear into the gloom above.

Staring at them, Jack realized that these tentacles were clamped immovably to the bare rock with gigantic metal bands. Gulping, he looked more closely at the body of the creature — and realized that it was surrounded by cables, tubes, and ducts whose purpose he could not guess, but which cocooned its titanic body and penetrated deep into its flesh.

The creature was attended by robed Collectors who swarmed above and around it on ledges and walkways, adjusting valves and relays, making notes on clipboards. They looked like vigilant nurses surrounding an unconscious patient in an intensive care unit. But the creature wasn't unconscious. As he gazed at the terrible, pitiable entity imprisoned in the cavern, Jack was conscious of a great wounded mind, reaching out to him. . . .

H e l p M e . . .

The slow, sad, pain-filled voice echoed silently in Jack's mind.

"It's horrible," Merle said faintly. "It's disgusting."

"It's intelligent." Jack swung to face the Master, clenching his fists. "And it's in agony!" The Master regarded him silently.

Tracer clicked his forked tongue. "You're right. I'm afraid the Collectors really aren't very nice people."

The elephant-eared alien peered down at the suffering colossus with casual interest. "You see, there are all kinds of life-forms in the Galaxy. They all need somewhere to live and something to eat. Some life-forms live in very unusual places and eat very interesting things.

"Take this life-form. It evolved here, in the heart of a planet. Of course, no other animals lived down here, and no plants could grow. So it survived by feeding off subspace energy, which washes around the Galaxy like ripples on a pond.

"The creature survived — but just barely. But then advanced life-forms began to evolve. The radio waves generated by their primitive communications equipment began to wash through the Galaxy. They increased the energy and frequency of the subspace waves. The creature fed and grew.

"But while it lay hidden within Helios, different life-forms were also evolving on the planet's surface: crafty, despicable humanoid creatures, who became successful by ruthlessly exploiting their environment, bless their hard little hearts." Tracer wiped away a sentimental tear. "While mining the planet for precious ores, they discovered this creature."

"Why didn't they just get rid of it?" asked Loaf. Jack and Merle shot him disgusted looks.

Tracer gave Loaf a bright smile, like that of a master to a promising pupil. "At first, they had plans to. But they gradually came to realize that by tapping into the signals the creature absorbed to sustain its life they could monitor everything that happened in the Galaxy, eventually becoming possessed of all knowledge. Therefore, they called themselves the Collectors."

"So they collect knowledge as well as handouts." Merle sniffed. "Well, I guess everyone should have a hobby."

Bitz bared his teeth. "Most beings manage to collect knowledge without keeping other beings imprisoned to do it."

"Oh, I don't know," said Tracer. "I've always found brutal incarceration a most efficient means of gaining information quickly." It indicated the miles of pipes and cables. "The measures the Collectors took succeeded in speeding up the processing time in which the creature could absorb signals. They discovered that its sensory organs were in the tips of its tentacles. So they dragged those to the surface." Tracer pointed at the creature's limbs, heartlessly manacled to the jagged rocks of its prison. "Then they entombed each limb in a column of marble, from which they created their Temple of the Five Winds."

"Then the temple," said Jack slowly, "is really a kind of antenna?"

"Yes. All such temples throughout the Galaxy are communications devices." Tracer gave Jack a patronizing smile. "I believe several were abandoned long ago on your homeworld. The people who found them thought they were places where humans might communicate with the supernatural." Tracer shrugged. "And they were, in a way.

"But we were talking about the Collectors. Eventually, they created a vast computer to interface with the creature. The room in which you met me lies at the heart of that computer. The Collectors called the combined brain of the creature and computer Tiresias."

Jack directed a look of utter contempt at the Master, whose face remained impassive.

The Collector said, "We are Collectors of information. We seek only enlightenment."

"Well, hooray for you." Merle had overcome her horror for the living part of Tiresias when she realized its plight. "Tell me, O enlightened one, what do you do with all this knowledge?"

The Master looked puzzled. "Do? One does nothing with enlightenment. Achievement is all."

Merle's eyes flashed. "Do you mean to tell me," she grated, "that you have tortured that poor creature down there for hundreds of years . . ."

"Thousands," corrected Tracer cheerfully.

Merle closed her eyes for a moment. "For thousands of years," she amended, "and you've kept it imprisoned and in pain all that time, and it's given you information — information about how to end wars and cure diseases and prevent disasters and help people understand one another better — and you've collected all that information and you've never *done* anything with it?!"

The Master stared at Merle as if she had gone crazy.

Once more, the captive creature's thoughts ran through Jack's mind.

They fill me with knowledge from every star in the Galaxy. I know all. But I am blind. I have never seen the reality of all I know. I have never seen the sun or the sky. I have never seen those stars.

Jack said slowly, "Tiresias. The sightless one that sees all."

Tracer, unaware of Tiresias's communication with Jack, gave him a surprised look. "Indeed. Of course, that description could also apply to me." Tracer indicated his VR visor. "Very ironic, don't you think?"

"Yeah," said Merle cuttingly. "You slay me."

"All in good time. And now," Tracer continued, "I think I've satisfied your curiosity. Down to business. Somewhere in Tiresias's database is the clue that will lead me to The Weaver. But Tiresias, for all its vast accumulation of knowledge, is primitive and slow — hardly state of the art. That is why I need The Server, which you have obligingly brought to me. It contains details of Friends agents throughout the Galaxy. By matching these details with Tiresias's knowledge, I shall use The Server's processing capacity and speed to sift through the data to reveal the identity of The Weaver."

Jack clutched The Server to his chest. "I won't let you have it."

Tracer waved a negligent claw toward Merle. "Kill her."

Jack's resistance crumbled as one of the Bugs leveled an energy weapon at Merle. "All right!" With a trembling hand, he passed The Server to Tracer. The elephant-eared being took the device with an ironic bow and plugged a communications cable from the nearest console into its scuffed casing.

"There you go," said Merle, her voice dripping scorn. "Take it and go running back to The Tyrant like a good boy. He *will* be pleased."

Tracer, closely watching The Server's screen as the download of information from Tiresias began, grinned a strange, twisted smile. "Oh, you underestimate me, my dear. So does The Tyrant." Tracer's thin face turned a deeper shade of green, and his mean lips quivered. "Do you really think that once the most powerful device in the whole Galaxy is in my hands, I shall be anyone's *messenger*?" Tracer gave a dreadful cackle. "Oh, no, my poor deluded friends. I shall destroy The Weaver — I alone. And who will be The Tyrant then?"

The Bugs glanced at one another in confusion. But they were trained to be obedient and not to think. The energy weapons covering Jack and the others never wavered.

Time stood still. All sound seemed to stop in the cavern, except for the demented shrieks of laughter from the victorious Tracer. At length, a message formed on The Server's screen:

Download Complete

With a supreme effort of will, Tracer controlled himself. His visor glinted, and rivulets of drool ran down his chin as he tapped triumphantly at The Server's keyboard. "It is done!" he cackled. "All of Tiresias's knowledge is mine!" He threw his six arms wide. "I shall be the greatest power in the Galaxy! Even The Tyrant shall bow down before me!"

Help appeared, shimmering into holographic existence above The Server's keyboard, and gave Tracer a grin of pure malevolence. "Hey, Tracey! How're ya doin'? I got a message for ya!"

Tracer stopped gloating and stared at Help. The smug creature seemed, for once, at a loss. "A message? For me? Who from?"

Help leered. "Search me. The Weaver maybe? That's the guy you were lookin' for, isn't it?" With a cackle, the hologram faded.

The Server's screen cleared. A face began to form.

CHAPTER TEN

As the face took on a recognizable form, Tracer made a shocked noise, something between a hiss and a gasp. His whole body became rigid, and his limbs trembled uncontrollably. "This is madness! I haven't ordered The Server to begin the search for The Weaver yet! And even if I had, it couldn't have processed the data so quickly!"

Bitz gave a joyful bark. "Janus?!"

Tracer indicated the screen with three shaking claws. "What nonsense is this? That being cannot be The Weaver."

Loaf was baffled. "If Janus is The Weaver, why did he keep telling us to get The Server to The Weaver if he was The Weaver all the time?"

"Janus isn't The Weaver," said Bitz. "I've

known him all my life. Great guy, but he couldn't weave a basket. Something else must be happening."

Janus moved his index finger, leaving a glowing trail on the screen that formed into letters:

Sorry . . .

Janus blew on the letters, which disappeared. Then he wrote:

. . . I need your Server.

Tiresias's cavern was engulfed in a vast, muted explosion. Crashing blue waves of pure energy washed over the creature's surface. Streams of blue fire crackled along the cables and connectors that chained Tiresias. The Collectors screamed and ran for their lives to escape the surging power. Sparks fizzled from the probes and power cables surrounding the creature's body. The Bugs stared in horrified confusion as the whole cavern was inundated with flashes of pure particle energy.

"No!" screamed Tracer. He reached for The Server with twitching claws in a desperate attempt to break the connection between it and Tiresias.

However, the instant the cable became unplugged from its socket in The Server, a stream of plasma energy shot from it, maintaining the connection. Tracer lit up like an X ray and was thrown onto the floor. He lay clutching at his VR visor, which had turned black, its circuitry burned out.

"I can't see," he cried. "I'm blind!"

Amid the turmoil, Jack dashed to The Server and snatched it up. He turned to the others and gasped. His companions, the Master Collector, and the Bugs were caught in an expanding blue-white vortex. The cavern seemed to be melting away. The fabric of reality began to unravel before Jack's eyes. Everything was a blur as his surroundings tore apart and imploded into a kaleidoscope of individual particles.

Then there was silence.

Jack found himself standing still in a universe of movement that ebbed and flowed, sparkled and shimmered. The reality from which he had come had faded into near invisibility. Around him, glittering particles and flaring waves of energy flowed in incomprehensible patterns, forming microscopic galaxies that were destroyed and re-created in the blink of an eye. Photons and electrons tripped the light fantastic, crashing into one another and wheeling apart in the wild steps of a microcosmic dance.

Jack reached out to touch the streams of color. It was as if he was grasping liquid metal. Ripples of light oscillated and spun away as his touch disturbed the very fabric of the universe.

Standing before him, he could make out the shapes of his companions, but their bodies were transparent, and their only reality seemed to be the pulses of electrical energy that constantly flowed along their nerve fibers, from the outermost extremities to the glowing fires of their brains.

A vast, ill-defined shape hung above, below, and all around them: Slower and more powerful pulses of coherent energy flowed through the numberless cells, relays, and semiconductors of the vast composite creature called Tiresias.

Out of the flux another figure began to materialize. The ethereal form became more substantive. Jack's heart leaped. It was Janus!

Jack tried to speak. Particles of pure matter poured out from his mouth, vibrating the surrounding elements.

W h e r e **N S p a c e** a r e w e ?

The answer came to him even as he asked the question. This was N-space. More questions sprang to his mind, but as he tried to communicate them, he found that he already knew the answers. Question and answer became one. Jack tried to share this insight with his friends. But then he realized that they already understood, just as he was aware of what the others were thinking even before the thought had occurred to them.

The confusion was overwhelming. Jack found no sense or discernible pattern in his surroundings. All was chaos. Perhaps, like a magic-eye picture, if he stared at the turmoil for long enough, he would be able to make out a picture in the formless colors. He closed his eyes and concentrated on putting his mind in order, trying to pick out one relevant thought and ignoring the rest. . . .

Suddenly, he found himself sitting on a hard plastic chair, staring at a chipped Formica tabletop. Around the table sat Merle, Loaf, Googie, Bitz . . . and Janus.

Jack stared around. They appeared to be the only customers in a snack bar. Above the service counter was a menu promising tempting delights, most of which involved meat in buns with fries. But no one was serving.

"Janus!" Bitz put his front paws on the table. His tail wagged furiously.

"Wow! Neat!" Loaf's voice was enthusiastic. "Can I get a burger and a shake here?"

"I'm afraid not," said Janus. "What you see around you is not real. I have created it. It is merely a projection of the mind. I thought you might find familiar surroundings more comfortable. I took this image from the memory of one of you."

Merle glanced around. "Loaf's?"

Janus looked puzzled. "Yes. How did you know?"

"Who else thinks about food *all* the time?"

"So where are we?" asked Jack.

Janus gestured at the strange universe beyond the windows of the "snack bar." "We are in N-space."

Jack was confused. "I thought nothing existed in N-space."

"Matter, as we understand it, does not exist here," explained Janus. "N-space is a place beyond comprehension. A place where what has been, what is, and what will be all exist at the same moment. It is a region of reality without substance, a place of possibilities and potentials."

"But how did we get here?" Jack wanted to know. "One minute, Tracer was downloading Tiresias's memory . . ."

"It was with Tiresias's assistance that I was able to bring you here." Janus paused as their surroundings were illuminated by bright flashes of energy from beyond the "windows" of their refuge. Janus smiled. He looked beyond the bubble of unreality in which they sat and raised his voice, as though speaking to someone outside. "Tiresias, my Friend, I thank you. You have done well."

Another surge of energy flashed through the insubstantial fabric of N-space. The companions stared at one another as each felt a sensation of joy ripple through their consciousness.

"Tiresias?" asked Jack.

"Tiresias is happy to have been able to assist you. We have been in contact with each other for some time." Janus frowned. "It is difficult to explain. In N-space there are energies that are unperceived in our universe. Thought becomes energy, energy becomes thought. That is how I was able to contact you through The Server on your return from Deadrock and guide you to Helios, to complete this part of your quest."

Jack stared at Janus. "Then you know everything that's happened to us?"

"In N-space, many things are known."

"Did you know that Tracer would be at Helios?" asked Loaf.

"Yes."

Merle gave Janus an angry look. "Then why send us there?"

"Because you had to meet with Tiresias," explained Janus. "As I told you, the sightless one will help you find The Weaver. Before Tiresias's knowledge was downloaded into The

Server, I was able to communicate with you only in the most fragmentary way. Now, as you see . . ." Janus gestured at their surroundings, "such meetings can be managed more easily. And without Tiresias's knowledge, you will not be able to fulfill your mission."

"Does Tiresias know who The Weaver is?" asked Jack.

"Some things are hidden even from Tiresias," said Janus. "And also from me," he added, anticipating Jack's next question.

"What do we have to do?" asked Bitz.

"Tiresias has passed his knowledge into The Server. One piece of information is crucial. It will enable you to save The Server from falling into the clutches of the FOEs."

"We already have," Googie pointed out acidly. "Plenty of times."

"This is different." Janus's voice allowed for no argument. "You must return to the past to save The Server — to the time when Sirius and I first rescued it, and perhaps beyond."

"You mean time travel?" said Bitz. "The Server doesn't do time travel. . . ."

"It didn't," said Janus. "But Tiresias has downloaded this knowledge into its processors. That is why I sent you to Helios. Now you will be able to journey in time in order to save the Galaxy. When you deliver The Server to The Weaver, he will be able to use this new knowledge to defeat The Tyrant."

Jack then asked the question that had nagged him from the beginning of the quest. "Why me? Why us?"

"It has to be someone," replied Janus. "It was not coincidence that The Server found you on Earth, Jack. You are not a stranger to it. All of you are involved in this quest."

"Loaf, too?" asked Merle. "Tracer will still be able to control him through that tracking device."

The others looked at Loaf. His skin became transparent. A deep crimson mass pulsed at the base of his brain. Janus thrust out his hand in a commanding gesture. A stream of energy sparkled from his fingers, hitting the device and atomizing it instantly.

"That problem is solved," said Janus. "Tracer's control is no more."

Bitz stared at his former companion. "What will happen to Tracer? Is he dead?"

"He has his part still to play," said Janus.

"You will meet with him again. But now, you must return to the Galaxy of normal space. You will repay my debt to Tiresias."

Bitz looked dismayed. "Us? What about you? Aren't you coming with us?"

Janus shook his head sadly. "I summoned your consciousness into N-space for the purpose of this meeting, but your bodies remain on Helios. Mine no longer exists, so I must remain here." Bitz lowered his head onto his front paws and whined. "Perhaps, one day I shall find a way to return." Janus gave Bitz an encouraging smile. "But for now, we have different paths to follow. I will do my best to guide you by delivering instructions from N-space." Janus held up one hand and closed his eyes. "Say nothing and you will understand. Open your minds."

There followed a moment of silent communication.

Janus relaxed. "It is done." He made the Friends secret signal and disappeared leaving a single thought. "Go well."

The snack bar vanished. The pulsing energies of N-space faded.

Jack blinked and looked around. He and his

companions stood once more on the surface
of Helios, in the center of the Temple of the
Five Winds.

Jack exchanged glances with the others,
but there was no need for explanations. All
knew what they had to do.

Each of the Friends made their way to a
column, placed a hand or paw on the cool
marble surface, and stared out and up into the
night sky.

Each of them felt a deep pulse from within
their chosen column as they made a connection with Tiresias. They became eyes for the
creature. For the first time, the sightless one
saw what it had been denied throughout its
existence.

From deep within their minds, the soul of
the imprisoned creature cried out in wonder.

I never knew it was so beautiful.

The companions gazed into the infinite
reaches of the heavens, awestruck at the
majesty and beauty of the cosmos. Uncount-
able stars dazzled and shimmered, innumer-
able nebulae glowed with every color of the
spectrum. Beyond these, millions of light-

years away, were the echoes of other galaxies, other stars, other worlds, and other beings. Tiresias saw and felt them all.

The creature radiated joy and sadness.

I see everything and I realize I know nothing.

The sky lightened and the stars winked out as the first of the Helian suns rose slowly above the horizon in a burst of orange and gold.

Thank you, my Friends, for showing me this. My life is fulfilled.

The pulse grew slower and softer, until finally, the quietest of murmurs spilled from the columns and was borne away by the wind.

Thank you . . .

The pulse died out. All was silence.

Jack tightened his grip on the column. Across the stone rectangle, Merle's faint sobs could be heard. Jack's lip quivered, and he wiped the tears from his face. Even Loaf was stung into reflection.

Bitz was the first to break the connection. He pattered slowly to the edge of the temple. Silhouetted against the disk of the rising sun, he raised his head and let out a heart-wrenching howl for Tiresias, Janus, and all beings that knew death.

A deep rumble came from below them. The columns shook.

"We have to go back to the past," said Jack firmly, "as Janus told us." He held up The Server. "If we don't rescue this from the FOEs, everything that's happened since The Server arrived on Earth won't have happened, so we won't be standing here and I won't be saying this, and we won't be able to save the Galaxy from The Tyrant."

"True, if confusing," said Googie. "Interesting paradox."

Further speculation was cut off by the appearance of Help. "What is goin' on here?" demanded the hologram. "Who auto-dumped all this data? There's so much stuff inside here, I can hardly move! What am I, some kinda warehouse?"

"That information will enable us to go back in time," explained Jack.

The hologram burst into a cackle. "Haaaaaa. You are delusional! Time travel?

Time travel don't happen in this galaxy, kludge-brain. Time travel don't . . ."

"Check it out," Merle interrupted.

"Okay, okay, monkey-mind." As Help took an inventory of The Server's files, his jaw dropped lower and his eyes grew wider. "You will not believe what I've got in here now!" The hologram's mouth watered in excitement. "Oh, are we gonna have some fun. I can set coordinates for any time! Where d'you want to go today? Or yesterday?"

"I think you'll find that there's a set of coordinates already programmed in," said Jack.

Help frowned. "How do you know?"

"We know," said Merle.

Help eyed the group, eyebrows raised. They all nodded.

"Will someone please tell me what's going on here? How come you know more than me? That's not supposed to be in the script."

"Think of it as bringing some excitement into your life," smiled Jack, recalling Help's comment on board *Trigger*. He looked toward the others. "Are you ready for the next part of this mission?"

They all nodded.

"Time travel. You think this is going to work?" asked Merle.

Jack shrugged. "There's only one way to find out."

He pressed SEND.

As the travelers disappear, the ground shakes. The doors of the Temple of the Five Winds open. Panic-stricken Collectors stream out.

On a hill, a wizened old man dressed in plain brown robes leans on a staff overlooking the temple. He extends one hand and opens it. A green butterfly rests on his flattened palm.

Gently, the old man blows on the butterfly. It flaps its wings.

The old man gazes at the temple. The butterfly's wings beat faster. Before the Collectors' thunderstruck gaze, the columns topple.

The old man nods with approval.

"Confusion is confused, is he? Ha!"

The butterfly flutters to his shoulder and rests there. The old man turns his back on the ruined temple and, leaning heavily on his stick, hobbles away, down the hill and out of sight.

**There's something out there . . .
And it's the next**

#4 time out

A series of blinding blue-white flashes shot through the dripping forest canopy. As these faded, five figures formed from the after-image and looked cautiously around.

"Teleportation is the worst," complained Loaf. He stretched and stared at the lush vegetation that surrounded the traveling companions. Huge trees reached into the darkness above and hundreds of tree creepers and vines dangled down from the giant branches that stretched out across the darkening sky.

"Looks like we're in the middle of a forest," said Jack.

"Well spotted, man-cub." Loaf applauded sarcastically. "But what are we doing here?"

Jack nodded toward the black laptop computer in his hands. "Getting The Server to The Weaver like Janus said."

"Yeah, yeah, we know," said Loaf sourly,

"so The Weaver and the Friends can defeat The Tyrant and the FOEs, and blah blah blah." He glared angrily at The Server. "That thing keeps teleporting us into every trouble-spot around the Galaxy looking for The Weaver, and we don't know who or what The Weaver is, or even whether he really exists at all. I'm starting to think there ain't no such thing. Yeuch!"

Somewhere above, a leaf had tipped and sent a stream of chilly water cascading down the back of Loaf's neck. He wriggled inside his suddenly damp New York Giants shirt, and swore. "And this place doesn't look any better than the other low-rent neighborhoods we've ended up in." He looked around apprehensively. "Too many trees, too many shadows. There could be anything in there."

"Such as?" purred the cat winding itself around Merle's legs.

Loaf glared down at Googie. "Such as giant *ann-ie-con-das* that wrap themselves around their prey — like cats, for instance — and squeeze them until their brains come out of their ears like toothpaste from a tube."

Googie gave him a contemptuous glance.

"Anacondas live in South America, and this is not Earth." Nevertheless, she stayed close to Merle.

Merle shook her head. "I don't think this *is* a forest, as we know it. It looks like some giant botanical garden. Look at those." She pointed toward a series of walkways suspended high above the forest floor. Beyond these, nestled among the trees, were several transparent domes that glowed with internal lights.

Jack looked down at the small dog at his feet. "Any ideas, Bitz?"

Bitz gave a doggy grin. "We must be in dog heaven. Look at all those trees!" His rear leg twitched and a thread of saliva dribbled from his mouth.

"You are so *basic*," spat Googie, licking her paw. "Never mind where we are, have the FOEs got a trace on us?"

Jack shrugged. "I don't know, but The Server can tell us. Help!"

Ching!

A silver holographic head shot out of The Server and shimmered over the keyboard. "Kludge! That trip has phase-changed my circuits!"

"What's the problem?" asked Loaf.

"There's no problem, monkey-brain," snapped Help. "It just so happens that I've never done time travel before, and I've got some polymorphic kludges messing up my innards."

Jack stared at the hologram. "So we've actually traveled back in time?"

"You'd better believe it," replied Help. "We've just undergone a time-teleportation experience through the courtesy of t-t-mail. And that wasn't a stutter."

"So where are we?"

"*When* are we?"

"Hey, one at a time! We *were* on planet Helios, we're *now* on Vered II, a forest planet in the Eridanus system. Lucky for you primates, there's plenty of trees for you to climb and leaves to wipe your . . ."

"Hold on a cotton-pickin' minute!" Bitz was staring at the hologram. "Vered II? You have to be kidding me! This can't be Vered II — that's where Janus and me found The Server before we came to Earth. It didn't look anything like this!"

Help frowned ferociously. Hologrammatic

steam poured from his ears. "Listen, dog-breath, are you calling me a liar?!"

"Lighten up," interrupted Merle. "Maybe you're both right. How far back in time have we come?"

Help gave Bitz another filthy look as it calculated. "At a rough estimate, about a hundred Gala-years."

Merle shrugged. "There you go. A place can change a lot in a hundred years."

"Not that much," muttered Bitz, looking unhappy and unconvinced.

"Have the FOEs got a trace on us?" demanded Googie. "Do they know we're here?"

"Give me time," muttered Help. The hologram's eyes spun around for a second or two. "No. There's nothing. I can't locate any kind of Outernet signal from Friends or FOEs."

"How can that be?" asked Merle.

"We've gone back," replied Help, "to a time before the Outernet existed. . . ."

About the Authors

Steve Barlow and Steve Skidmore

Steve and Steve are both humans of an indeterminate age who have been writing books for young life-forms for more than thirteen Earth years. They live in England with their pets, families, and other aliens. They are presently working on the Zargian version of Outernet but are finding the spelling very difficult.

About the Website

Creative Director: Jason Page
Illustration, design, and programming: Table Top Joe
Additional illustration: Mark Hilton
Script by Steve Barlow, Steve Skidmore, and Jason Page

About You

Once you've logged on to the Outernet, use this space to record your identification.

AGENT ID   _____
PASSWORDS _____
             _____
             _____

OUTERNET™

www.go2outer.net

ST. BARTHOLOMEW'S SCHOOL